LIES THAT BIND US

MISSION 13

BLACK OCEAN: PASSAGE OF TIME

J.S. MORIN

Magical Scrivener Press
www.magicalscrivener.com

Publisher's Note: This is a work of fiction. Names, characters, places, and incidents are a product of the author's imagination. Locales and public names are sometimes used for atmospheric purposes. Any resemblance to actual people, living or dead, or to businesses, companies, events, institutions, or locales is completely coincidental.

Ordering Information: Special discounts are available on quantity purchases by corporations, associations, and others. For details, contact the publisher at the address above.

J.S. Morin — First Edition

LIES THAT BIND US
MISSION 13

CAPTAIN JESSICA JUDITH RAMSEY stared down two of her officers over the rim of a coffee mug. A hangover hammered the walls of her skull from the inside, but that was the least of her concerns at the moment.

"So. Do either of you remember bridge duty training?"

Lt. Daphne Morgan and Lt. Mindy Sedgwick shared a furtive glance before each granting their captain a faint nod in the affirmative.

"And, when we covered the chain of command. What a duty officer is and is not authorized for. You were awake and listening for that portion, correct?"

"You see, ma'am, we just—" Mindy started but cut herself short.

Jessie raised a finger. She wasn't interested in excuses. "Yes or no?"

"Yes. Ma'am."

"Yes, ma'am," Daphne agreed.

Jessie nodded, taking a sip from her coffee. "Great. Now that we've established that, I'd like an explanation of the chain of events whereby you gave a civilian authorization to depart the *Arete* with a ship that didn't belong to him."

The pair squirmed under her scrutiny.

Mindy broke first. "He said you wanted him off the ship. Let us try to wake you up to check his story and everything."

Jessie held up a datapad. "Five text comms. I missed five text comms. So, that's the point at which you're willing to mutiny?"

Her two lieutenants appeared aghast.

"Mutiny?" Daphne echoed as if those giant azrin ears of hers hadn't heard clearly.

"Captain, we didn't—"

"Yes, you did!" Jessie snapped, instantly regretting the jabbing pain behind her eyes. "Since entering eyndar space, we've been on lockdown. No ships enter or leave without my personal authorization. And until Junior gets back from the *Scylla*, it's just Lisa and the two of you. Luckily for you both, I won't put Lisa in the position of being the only security officer aboard. Consider yourself reprimanded, and I'll be assigning you both remedial training in shipboard operations and protocols. Understood?"

The two answered in unison. "Yes, ma'am!"

Once they were gone from her ready room, Jessie allowed herself to slouch.

This was a hell of a way to wake up.

Eric was going to be pissed.

There was no way Jessie was going to comm Mom to tell her Carl had run off.

If Lisa was looking forward to having her ship back, she'd have to take it up with the thief herself.

And if Hadrian changed his mind about staying, Jessie didn't have any convenient way to get rid of him.

What a shit show.

What a clown fiesta she was running here.

What a splitting, freaking headache she had.

It was tempting to head down to Med Bay. Harmony could fix this in seconds. But the ship's chief medical officer had disabled the features that would keep Jessie from enjoying alcohol at all—at her own insistence. Coffee and a headache were a small price to pay in comparison.

Jessie's bigger headache was her father.

He wasn't answering comms, either.

It was plain as a lone ship in the astral. He *hadn't* known about Aunt Jamie. She'd replayed as much of the dinner conversation from the previous night as she could recall, and there was no proof. At the time, knowing Aunt Jamie's wife's name seemed like solid evidence—Jessie supposed that Sofia was an aunt, too, now that she considered it. But Carl had just made an inference. His anecdote about Aunt Jamie trying to set the two of them up implied that he already knew her. The rest was unverifiable drivel and easy assumptions.

Jessie choked down an angry gulp of coffee, kept hotter than advisable to gulp by her induction mug. Her self-punishment for gullibility.

That was why there was a limit to her punishment for Daphne and Mindy. Carl had fooled better, more suspicious minds than theirs. It was unfair of her to assume they had what it took to see through his lies.

She hadn't.

A lifetime of being a sucker. She'd known Carl was a liar. He'd admitted as much, taught her how to spot it in others, trained her to look out for herself in the cold, wide galaxy with her wits and her mouth. Mom was the one who'd taught her how to fly and shoot.

That had been yet another lie.

She'd grown up believing Mom was the top starfighter pilot

in Earth Navy. Turns out, she'd been raised by the top two, and Mom wasn't number one.

There were a million things Carl wasn't good at.

He couldn't cook. Couldn't sing. Couldn't play guitar worth a damn. Didn't know how to repair any damn thing on a starship. Lost money gambling. Cracked the lamest jokes. Barely made enough money to keep the *Mobius* fueled.

Dad was just this hapless, easy-going goofball who didn't take the galaxy too seriously, and she'd loved him as that.

At one point, right around the time she was taking an interest in the dumber sex, Jessie had asked her mother what she'd seen in Carl. The answer strongly implied a level of sexual prowess that kept the subject from ever coming up again.

But now that she had the full picture, it made sense in retrospect.

In his prime, Carl could shoot a 10T coin out of the air and have it land as a five and five ones. He was Earth Navy's all-time starfighter kill leader. He'd been an outlaw and was friends with the Convocation's number one most wanted fugitive. Carl was dangerous, smooth as ice, and—if Mom could be trusted as objective—packed equipment that it would be illegal to replicate in a pleasure pod.

She'd seen none of that.

He'd hidden it for over twenty years right in front of her. Sure, for some of that, she'd been a kid. For a lot of it, she had no excuse.

But Dad was an old man now. He'd caught wind of a ghost and a secret and had correctly assumed Jessie wasn't about to let him run off looking for his big sister, lost all these years. He'd run off without a plan or backup.

Maybe he *could* find Aunt Jamie on his own.

But Carl was her dad. And he was out in eyndar space.

Jessie worried about him.

The rendezvous between the *Arete* and the *Barton* had gone as well as could be expected. The Harmony Bay relief ship was straining at every seam with as large a load of passengers as the vessel's designers could possibly have imagined.

Harmony rode back with Grosstet at the controls of his own shuttle.

Captain Rousseau passed along regrets for not being there to see them off personally. Harmony would hear none of it.

The *Barton* had so much left to do, while Harmony looked forward to sleeping in her own bed that night.

Three days.

Three days of the *Arete* missing, lost in time.

Heartsick. Throwing herself into the task of securing refuge for over a hundred thousand humans. Worrying. Eric could have launched the *Arete* into the distant past or distant future. Jamie Ramsey's deception might have become a prophecy, for all Harmony knew.

But that was over now.

The *Arete* had returned. Harmony had spoken to Xrista on video comm. Captain Rousseau would depart soon for New Garrelon, delaying just long enough to ensure that his people got everyone settled and immediate medical problems sorted out; also to give the stuunji people time to prepare for so many new arrivals.

The welcome on the *Arete* was limp.

Makket and a few of his Logistics workers helped offload the shuttle and its passengers. There was repair work ongoing, left over from a battle that hadn't taken place that long ago for the *Arete* crew.

Harmony didn't even look for the gear she'd brought along for what had started out looking like a hijacking. Someone would take care of it. Or she'd look for it after a night's sleep. Whatever. She was past caring.

A lift ride and a zombie walk. Her steps quickened as she neared her quarters.

The door shushed open.

Harmony quieted her footsteps, slipping off shoes mid-stride. Xrista woke groggily when Harmony looked in on her.

"Mommy?"

The word that made it all worthwhile.

Harmony rushed over and gathered her daughter in a hug that verged on desperate. Somehow, amid a shower of affection reciprocated with semi-comatose instinct, she ended up seated in Xrista's bed with her lap as a pillow.

Much as she made an effort, and tired as she was, Harmony couldn't find a way to fall asleep like that. Not that she was uncomfortable. It just wasn't conducive to sleeping.

And, as beautiful as the girl on her lap might have been, staring at her all night was simply a recipe for a cramped neck and boredom.

Thankfully, Harmony rarely went anywhere without some kind of tech available to her. She pulled down the datagoggles atop her head and the retina scans logged her in.

Unblocking "comm silence" mode unleashed an avalanche. Everyone wanted a piece of her. From Harmony Bay directors to producers of galaxy-spanning newsfeeds. From Glastonbury Shipyard security to Mars Navy High Command. Her adaptive filters had detected a need and created a "Well-Wishes" sub-directory as well as sub-directories for "Martian Planetist Threats," "Offers to Join Crusade," and "Interview Requests." Apparently, certain GNN and MNN celebrities rated a double-classification to also appear in her high-priority inbox.

But, slogging through the requests and demands, Harmony

stumbled across a notification that had been tagged for her standing sift of anything regarding her moms' whereabouts.

Esper had given a press conference.

A little gasp escaped Harmony, and she froze when Xrista stirred at the sudden noise. Once the girl had settled back in, fully asleep, Harmony double-checked her audio settings to ensure she was on bone conduction only and loaded the feed.

Mom was looking a little worse for wear. Stress could do that. Ninety-nine percent of the galaxy wouldn't know the difference; her hair and cosmo people made sure of that—or Grace, if the family was together in exile without public relations support.

"My fellow Martians. My fellow humans. My fellow sentients everywhere, my name is Esper Richelieu, rightful president of Mars, currently in exile. It is at great personal risk that I record this message; Martian Dictatorial Government assassins will no doubt take heart as my present location is revealed. But I have just watched the reports from Ghenlar Par'Mol, and I cannot remain silent.

"I have nothing but respect and swelling pride for the brave crew of the relief ship Barton *and the tactical support that made the rescue effort a success.*

"But I have questions. How was such a large-scale operation kept under wraps? Who knew about this outside the Eyndar Empire? And why have they said nothing?

"I think I have answers to all three, though I like none. Who knew? Earth Navy Intelligence. Mars Navy Intelligence. Earth Interstellar. Phabian Investigative Services. I could go on, but the former ARGO intelligence and law enforcement agencies could NOT have been ignorant.

"How was it kept quiet? Complicity. Plain and simple. There have been treaties in place for generations now, forbidding the keeping of captive workers, regardless of species. Violations

would have led to renewed wars. But what good is peace if not to ensure the welfare of our people? We sacrifice the least fortunate among us to safeguard our armed forces? No. To safeguard the careers of politicians.

"That's the answer to why. Politics. Public sentiment. Maintaining the status quo. But many of you may note that the status quo has already shifted. Earth is still a tyrannical empire, and rather than providing a beacon of hope, Mars has slunk to those autocratic depths instead.

"And so, as the elected president of a free Mars and the rightful representative, I demand the immediate release of all captive workers within the Eyndar Empire and ongoing audits to ensure the practice does not resume."

The newsfeed cut away to pundits who focused on the revelation of Mom's exile on Poltid.

"And there we have it. Richelieu ends her hiding from Martian justice by broadcasting a Harmony Bay press release from Poltid, an insignificant member of the League of Independent Planets. Appropriate, given her present status as an insignificant factor in Martian politics."

"I think it's a real show of character that her first public statement since exile is PR damage control for her company. The blame-shifting narrative can't overshadow the terrorist attack on the Glastonbury Shipyard."

Gritting her teeth, Harmony switched to another feed.

"... if she thinks this will earn her a place at the table. Martians have spoken, and they overwhelmingly support the current military government to end the Earth crisis."

Harmony tried several more.

"... slick timing and carefully staged faux-low-budget presser..."

"... ... couldn't have come at a better time to disrupt preparation for Martian Independence Day celebrations..."

"... ... ... *could number herself among those complicit in the ongoing eyndar situation, if that was her motive...*"

"... ... ... *is really buying the concerned citizen act. This is just a hook to get her name back into—*"

Harmony shut off her goggles. The ambient feed of her blood pressure was reason enough, and her heaving breath threatened to wake the sleeping child in her lap.

Mom, and presumably Mom and her sisters, were apparently safe on Poltid. Kubu would look after them. No one wanted to land on the klemekoo homeworld without invitation. The residents could smell an unfamiliar creature through a meter of solid steel. The spirits of the planet spoke to their shamans. And while they didn't *generally* eat sentient creatures, it was always an option.

Meanwhile, Harmony had Xrista. They were safe on the *Arete*. That was what really mattered.

Mom was naive to think anyone on the galactic stage was going to listen to her. She should have kept her head down, looked after the family, and thought of some new way to satisfy that admirable—and maddening—urge to save the galaxy.

Family was what really mattered. Nothing else could matter more to Harmony than Xrista and her upcoming little sister—whom she'd really need to check in on. So long as her family was all right, Harmony would be free to live whatever life she chose.

The streets of Tenia Oto glowed neon through a nighttime drizzle. Brick and steel and holographs crowded around narrow strips of crumbling asphalt that pedestrians and ground-rollers had to share. Despite all species being equally welcome here, most of the people Carl Ramsey encountered were either human or eyndar.

And equally welcome meant equally unwelcome.

The Eyndar/ARGO Disputed Zone had never formally been eliminated. But even before ARGO itself broke up, parties from both sides had filtered back into the region to avoid being governed by either. Lawlessness was the law of the land. Gangs roamed free. Blasters were mandatory. Nobody brought their families.

Carl knew most of this because it was the list of reasons Amy wouldn't let him book Squadron 33 1/3 to play here.

The unfamiliar feel of one of the *Arete's* target range blasters at his hip, the gray hair, and the lack of imposing physical stature didn't deter him from walking the Tenia Oto streets like he'd lived here his whole life. He didn't gawk at the eyndar peep shows being advertised or glance up every time a hover raced low overhead. He didn't pay attention to the catcalls and offers of stim and other drugs being peddled.

Carl Who Knew This Place didn't fall for any of that crap.

Tenia Oto mostly used terras as currency. Hell, even the League did, these days. No one respected marbits, and no one trusted a banag to be worth its printed value even in eyndar space, let alone beyond its fringes.

Light on hardcoin, Carl scammed a side-alley three-card-monte dealer out of 500T. Betting with no cash to cover his guess, he made eye contact with the dealer and mouthed "left palm" before announcing his pick to a gathered crowd. Rather than having his trick revealed to a mixed crowd of xenos less familiar than Carl with human culture, the dealer paid up.

From there, Carl went clubbing.

The sign meant nothing to him. Overly stylized, he wasn't even sure what language it had been written in. Carl declined the offer of a cranial electrode band at the door. Inside, thumping music and mixed-species dancers all wearing the neuro-block tech gave him vertigo just observing. He pushed his way through a crowd. Some of the drinks smelled familiar enough that he might have tried one if this had been a leisure trip.

Instead, he braved the audiovisual orgy and came out the far side, where booths and tables allowed less frolicsome patrons to watch and drink. Other than co-op dance jamborees in the colonial slums, every club had a section like this. Sometimes they were on a VIP upper level. Sometimes they clustered in the center of a donut of debauchery. Other times, like here, they were just off the far side of the action, like someone had cleared a few tables out of a McKenna's Steakhouse to put in a dance floor.

And Carl knew the kinds of people who came to watch.

"Don't recognize you," a fellow with an old-school Martian accent called out to him as Carl passed a table of besuited gentlemen and less-thoroughly-attired lady companionship. An azrin mercenary loomed, strapped with blasters and knives when he could have ripped Carl to shreds with his bare claws.

"Passing through," Carl Who Worked for a Syndicate told them. "Business."

The lead guy shook his head. "Nah. Boss woulda mentioned if anyone like you had business around here." He was skinny and smooth-faced, like someone who'd gotten gene-edited just to avoid shaving. A chronic squint narrowed his eyes, making them look both suspicious and disdainful at once.

"Probably means I don't have business with *you*," Carl replied easily. "Think that works well for both of us, wouldn't you say?"

The local gangster shook his head. "I don't like the look of this guy. Get him out of here."

Before the azrin bodyguard could lay a hand on him, Carl

stated simply, "That wouldn't work out as good for you. Who do you work for?"

"We're with Angelo Dyson. Better remember that name."

Carl did just that. "This is where Angelo landed? Small galaxy." How many Dysons could there be in the galactic criminal underworld? He didn't remember any Angelo, but he was well out of date with keeping up with Tanny's relatives. Dyson was her mother's maiden name. Her cousin Chip flew with them a while before offing himself in a freak plasma-torch accident. "Shame how Mars went down."

"Who the fuck are you?" the leader demanded.

Still in his persona of a syndicate captain on family business, Carl answered succinctly, "If you're really lucky, I'm nobody. I'm just on Tenia Oto for the answer to one question, and then I'll never have been here at all."

With a setup like that, and the lack of outward concern about getting manhandled by an azrin twice his size, how could these guys *not* at least find out?

"What question?"

"Where can I find the captain of the starship *Scylla*?"

Eric lay at the summit of a grassy mountain. His head brushed the top of another, prettier head as he stared into a blue sky filled with whimsical clouds.

Unlike many a lazy cloudwatch, he and Charlotte weren't trying to decide what images presented themselves. They were telling stories.

Each cloud became a balloon animal, a vehicle, a puppet. Their sky was a piece of Greek pottery, slowly rotating with the breeze and spinning a tale.

Two tales, really.

Mixing them was the main challenge.

Eric's contributions were singing animals and a happy-go-lucky travelogue of magical vistas. Charlotte, meanwhile, seemed intent on a tragic backstory and escaping from monsters.

Yet somehow, it was working.

In the valley below, daydreamy villagers would watch these skies for hours, forgetting chores and leaving crops to ripen an extra day before harvest. They hadn't named their home Skydream for nothing, after all.

A climatonomer had once tried to convince them that mountains tended to coerce clouds to drop snow. Or not cross mountains at all. Eric had really stopped paying attention once the guy admitted to his science bias.

But clouds rose much higher than mountains. And if they stopped clouds from crossing, then eventually all the clouds would be on one side and that would just look silly.

Instead, regardless of how they worked in the world outside, these clouds gave hope and wonder and sparked imagination. In all of the Village of Eternity, few places turned out as many artists as Skydream.

This particular world had other villages, towns, and even large cities where people could live easier, more comfortable lives. Yet a certain ilk collected in this sleepy fjord village, fishing and farming and repairing boats and whatever else fishing villages required, all for the chance to be inspired by this spectacle.

Farmers became sculptors—or sculptors paused farming to work.

Fishers set up easels in the fields.

Merchant musicians closed shops to compose scores and play open-air concerts to accompany a live cloudscape.

"I wish I could share this with more people," Eric mused as he loosed a bicycle-riding pig upon the heavens.

"You're reaching your limits," Charlotte reminded him. "Two worlds crumbled with the last new one we made."

"Yeah, but what if we started connecting them to your mind, too?"

He felt the shaking of Charlotte's head as it rubbed his scalp. "I've added an attic and a back room, but my bookshop is too tiny to make a difference. And I fear I'll never learn those crooked runes of yours. It's like fingerpainting with broken glass."

Eric winced at the vivid notion, curling his hands to protect tender fingertips from injury.

"Unless you're thinking to rope Hadrian or Sparta into this."

"Well..." This was a delicate topic to begin with. Charlotte's instant dislike of Hadrian's girlfriend wasn't going to help matters.

"Hadrian is an oaf. A stronger oaf than when he left us, surely, but an oaf nonetheless. And Sparta *is* a seer. She can't hide it. Doesn't even deny the fact. And why should she? These are lawless stars we find ourselves amongst. And until she predicts a gruesome death that comes to pass, no one will mind her little spoilers for the crew's futures. But give her a realm such as this, and you're liable to see things you don't wish to know."

"OK. Fair, but maybe Hadrian—"

"I daresay I can predict *his* imagination. Unfettered debauchery. A terrestrial mirror of my mother's flagship, redone in Oxford red brick and wrought iron and ivy. Collegiate admirers, unclad and throwing themselves his way. I don't know whether Sparta might dampen that inclination or whether she'd leap at the chance to flaunt her gaudy jewels without clothing to distract from them."

"I..." Eric found himself at a loss. This wasn't what he was suggesting. And she didn't know Hadrian at all. At least... Eric was *pretty certain* he knew the guy a lot better. *A lotta* lot better. "You know what? Forget I said anything. Let's get back to making an unforgettable cloud story for the Skydreamers."

Sometimes, it was easier to let someone you love win an argument rather than reveal a universe-grade secret that might get you both turned to ash.

... even if Hadrian probably *could* teach Charlotte how to make places like this.

"This will do for now."

Hadrian tried to hide the relief he felt at those words. He flopped into an armchair of unknown provenance and motioned for Sparta to join him in its mismatched counterpart on the far side of their dining table. "I know it's a lot to ask, but we should take a light hand with the overhauls."

Sparta smoothed her robes out of the way and sat. "I know I gave you a hard time when it came to the care and maintenance of a living space, but I hadn't imagined your predecessor lacked both self-esteem *and* taste."

"That's our emperor you're talking about," Hadrian pointed out her with a smirk.

Sparta groaned. "Don't remind me. And besides, are we really beholden to anyone out here? That haathee gentleman, I suppose?"

Hadrian matched her grunt with a harrumph. "Just met him. Already know the type. A gadabout know-nothing who likes being the center of attention. What better place for him than a slice of galaxy where his ignorance is insight and he's a one-man sideshow wherever he goes? Hear he makes a good brew, though, so I'm willing to give the guy a chance."

"How magnanimous of you," Sparta joked back at him.

Hadrian crooked a finger and summoned a footlocker with a comforter draped over it, which the previous occupant of the room had deemed an ottoman. He threw his feet atop it as it scraped across the floor and settled into position. After a sigh, Sparta placed her feet atop the far end of the cumbersome furnishing.

"I am the very picture of magnanimity. Not a single imbecile was maimed in the transfer of power. Not a dipshit so much as lost a job. I have availed myself of transport via an old friend who needed to get out of the house. I have taken on a job for which I am grossly overqualified and for which I will, very likely, not be paid."

"Point taken. And don't think that you're off the hook. We'll be antiquing for pirate chic come morning. And I'll be taking some time with those adorable squirrels to liven up our wardrobes a bit. The one who was helping us—"

"Tippitak," Hadrian supplied helpfully.

"Yes. She mentioned something about having chiffon in the science loom. Eric and Charlotte both have uniforms. We should as well."

"Do you anticipate joining the crew?" He honestly hadn't expected her to.

Sparta cocked her head. "I'd assume so. I've packed students off to war straight from undergraduate studies with less talent than you'd find in your average housecat. I may not be some mighty Promethean, but I'll keep a ship clear of magic for a few decks, at least. And should that Charlotte character overstep, I daresay I could squelch *her* feeble attempts to sway the universe."

"Better if you made nice. Eric's a good kid, and by all

accounts, she's a positive influence on him. Rare as snake feet for Carl to like someone his kids are seeing. Besides, I feel I owe her a chance, considering how close she came to never being born on account of me."

An old debate pro, he knew how to bait a hook. Sparta's eyes widened. "That's a tale I wouldn't mind hearing."

"Her mother's a pirate. Head pirate of an outfit that call themselves the Poet Fleet. They're hedonists with anachronistic fashion sensibilities; you'd like them."

"Would I, now?"

Hadrian's nod assured her that she would. "Once you set aside the murdering, raping, theft, hijacking, and drug smuggling, they're just a bunch of bookish thespians. Figured out how to enjoy the arts without megacorp day jobs. Frankly, it's not far off from what would happen if the Convocation were outlawed."

Sparta surveyed their quarters. Hadrian The Former had done little in the way of homemaking. And that little had been half undone. Furniture shifted. Certain trash had been left in the hallway for Logistics to reappropriate. Disposable silverware had been scooped from drawers and cupboards cleared of plastic cups. They'd washed the remaining three mugs and a lone, respectable plate fervently.

"It's big, at least."

"The size abounds."

"Bed seems far too tiny."

Hadrian nodded. "Indeed it does. Human furniture in a haathee-sized space."

"You willing to make me a princess tonight?"

Hadrian held her gaze. "I can make you a queen."

"Oh, I don't want a stuffy, stay-at-home king. I want a prince. We'll roam the countryside, fending off brigands and rescuing hapless villagers. And when night falls, we won't always circle back to the castle. We can stay at any inn we like, showering the proprietor with gold from the royal treasury and commanding the biggest room in the house. And it will have the teensiest little bed and—" Sparta couldn't finish through a fit of giggles.

It was late. They'd been on an adventure. Details and creature comforts could wait. All that mattered now was the little bed just big enough for both of them. Mortania awaited, and it was all they needed.

Comms didn't get better with age. And, in particular, comms to Mom didn't get better by blocking her comm ID and hoping she wouldn't try another.

Jessie Ramsey had learned this lesson five or six times over the course of her life, and it had, in the end, lodged firmly in place.

However, she found herself wishing she hadn't let this turn into a video comm.

"Yeah. I know. But he's *not* my responsibility."

"It's your ship, Jessica. Whether you own it or just operate it, you are the captain of the *Arete*. That means that anyone who comes aboard, from stowaway to VIP, prisoner to guest, is your responsibility. Any other place in the galaxy, you can argue that he isn't. But your father landed in your hangar, and you let him steal that fucking ship again and ion off to God-knows-where."

Mom had cut her hair short again. When Jessie was a kid, that usually followed some kind of household mishap that wouldn't have happened with shorter hair. Caught in the food processor? Time for a haircut. Ozzy pulling out a fistful trying to climb it like a rope? Time for a haircut.

Braids tangled into a strange infinite loop? Out came the scissors.

Frankly, Jessie wondered why Mom ever bothered letting it grow out. Then again, she'd done the same when she was trying to shed her in-the-barracks look for something more commanding respect.

But this pixie length didn't work. Jaw to shoulder was Mom's range, and Jessie was tempted to derail the conversation by bringing up haircare. Her autobiography would have an early chapter on diverting authority figures from the reason they're mad at you. Knowing the button to stop a core meltdown on Mom had been a key survival feature.

Learning how to fight back, and fight dirty, would be a later chapter.

"Oh. Care to pass along some motherly advice on how to nail Dad's feet to a planet or starship? Because Dad's still on New Garrelon where you left him, right? You *must* be an expert. Please. Enlighten me."

"You had him right there. All you needed to do was tell him, 'Enough is enough; Mom's worried about you. Go home.'"

"Yeah. That always works. Wait. Let me just play Dad here for a second. 'Oh, your mom worries too much. I'll be fine alone in eyndar space on my own.'" She did her Dopey Dad voice, but Mom wasn't laughing.

"He's... where?"

Jessie pursed her lips, instantly 14 again. "Um..."

"That wasn't hypothetical, was it?"

"I mean..."

"Did. Your. Father. Run. Off. In. Eyndar. Space?" Mom's teeth didn't unclench the entire time.

Jessie winced. The problem with parents was they threw off your entire energy. Normally, when she had someone on the other end of a comm, they saw Jessie as a badass. Starship captain. Special forces operative. Earth Navy officer, disgraced traitor, or otherwise.

It was hard maintaining that kind of vibe when the person on the other end remembered squeezing you out of her uterus and breastfeeding you. Diaper changes, crawling around trying to put random floor trash in her mouth, crying when she got hurt or scared or wasn't allowed to throw silverware in the waste reclaim to listen to the funny noises. Mom had seen it all, and she hadn't forgotten that dynamic.

"I want an answer, young lady."

"Yes."

"AND YOU LET HIM!?"

"Mom, come on! How was I supposed to know that he was lying when he said he already knew Aunt Jamie was alive and that as soon as my back was turned he was going to—"

"Who what now?" Mom's face had gone white and slack.

"Oh. I... I guess you didn't know either. But you never met her, right? So—"

"Carl's sister Jamie is alive? After all this time?" Oh, referring to Dad by his first name to Jessie was a bad sign. Even as a grown-ass woman, Jessie's mother always referred to him as her father or Dad.

"Yeah, well—"

"And when he acted smooth as cooking oil, played if off like he knew all along, you just... *believed* him?"

"I mean..."

"I know more about Jamie Ramsey than any person I've never met. Your father doesn't talk a lot about regrets in his life, but he does mention how different his life might have been if he'd taken your Aunt Michelle and run off to play Ramsey Family outlaws with the two of them. Says I'm the only reason he doesn't regret not doing it, and I'm not a hundred percent sure I believe him. So, if Jamie is alive and living in eyndar space somewhere, I'd recommend you find her and get the fucking reunion over with before that creaky, lovable old coot gets himself killed."

Jessie gulped. "Yes, ma'am. But she's gone dark. Some pirate shipyard she can't risk revealing."

Mom stared up into the heavens. "Of *course*, she's a pirate."

"No, no! Aunt Jamie hunts pirates. That news thingy. With the slaves. She helped. That was us. Her and us, I mean." Why did Mom fluster her to the point where she lost the power of cogent speech?

"Then why didn't *you* tell him in the first place?"

"She... asked me not to?" It sounded lame in retrospect. Now that Dad knew, obviously it would have been better to tell him rather than leave him in a room with Eric until Mr. Blabbermouth let it slip.

"Listen to me very carefully. You have commandeered yourself the most powerful starship in this half of the galaxy. You have a crew who, apparently, listen to you. You will take that ship and that crew and round up both your father and your aunt before anything tragic happens. I *will* see your father in person again. I *will* meet the mysterious Jamie. We *will* all have a nice holiday together this year as a big happy family. Do I make myself clear?"

"Yes, Mom."

"And remember to drink enough water, eat some vegetables, dress warmly, and keep strangers' dicks out of you. You know... all the usual stuff you never listened to. Love you."

"Love you too, Mom."

The comm winked out. Jessie sighed from her toes.

Other than her brief shuttle trip to the *Arete*, this was the first time Jamie Ramsey had spent any significant time off the *Scylla* in eons. Hypersensitive glass picked up every stray photon, allowing visitors on the observation deck to watch the ships being worked on in near-total darkness. As a priority customer and co-founder of the operation, Jamie got the place all to herself, watching the *Scylla* in the central bay, looking like a well-loved chew toy.

Serifos Supply Depot was a haven among havens. Carved out of rock, it drifted free in an abandoned asteroid mining operation. Ten thousand and more hunks of mineral debris, too worthless to bother harvesting any further, gave cover to the operation. A fleet of little tug-ships the size of planet-bound family hovers could sneak out and adjust its course if the need arose. One lone, retractable astral antenna could extend to listen for customers and respond with up-to-date coordinates.

At present, that antenna was retracted. The asteroid was a ghost. No one who didn't already know it was here would ever find it, and that list was vanishingly small.

Jamie puffed a stream of smoke, letting her mind and muscles relax. It was hard seeing the *Scylla* in this shape. But she couldn't not look. Her life depended on that ship doing exactly what she expected, exactly when she expected. The "when" came down to crew training, and that was tip-top. The "what" was in serious doubt until the vessel had a complete overhaul.

"Good, you're sitting down," her host greeted her upon entry to the observation deck. To even call it a "deck" was a stretch. Lounge, maybe. It had a scattering of plush chairs and one love seat, a few low tables that could support either snacks or feet, and a vending machine full of junk food that was set to zero for all prices. Hard to charge digital terras for anything without an omni connection.

"No honey, Kenny. Hit me with your worst," Jamie told him.

Kendek of Betelgeuse had more gray in his fur than last time Jamie had been here. He sported stained coveralls and worn walking gloves, despite being in charge of the whole operation. Ambling over, he transferred a datapad to his lower hands as he settled into a chair and took his gloves off.

"Well, let's see... Anything that might be considered an aerodynamic surface—which *should* be nothing on a deep-space craft like the *Scylla*—is toast. We're digging deep in our warehouse for the grade of plasticized steel you use, but we'll be replacing most of the outer hull. I told you those vish kinah don't know a damn thing about riv-welds."

"I can spot you a supply run once we're up and running again."

Kenny nodded. "Engines need a good refit and overhaul. Most of your power relays have irreparable damage—they'll work, but how long is a crapshoot. Most of your forward-facing glassteel is damaged but can be resurfaced. We've already adjusted a 0.6 degree offset in your gravity stone that wasn't present for your last visit. Probably knocked loose in whatever got you coming here."

Jamie would never have noticed that fine a misalignment of gravity with the ship's nominal "down" direction. "Fine. Take care of it all."

"You've got those nonstandard fuel rods, but we have enough in stock to take care of you. Med kit resupply. We can patch up a few cracks in your water and waste systems, flush the whole thing."

Jamie gave the mechanic a deadpan stare. "You're starting to sound like my doctor."

Kenny snickered and kept going. "Hydraulics have seen better days, but I don't think they need servicing. The way you treat ships, fresh actuators will look like your current ones in a month or two anyway."

"Anything else?"

Deft fingers flicked through screen after screen on the datapad. "Nah. Your people take as good care of the *Scylla* as anyone could be expected to without shipyard facilities."

"How much am I looking at?"

"Hmm... with the works... throw in a complimentary life support cleaning... let's call it 720,000 T."

"Done." Jamie tried not to let on how much that number hurt. Good ships cost less than that from a dealership. But no dealership worth their license was going to sell to Jamie Ramsey. Plus, as an investor in the place, about a quarter of that would be coming back to her.

"Your credit's good here, so we'll get on all that immediately." Jamie declined to point out that Kenny's people were already working on hull repairs. "That just leaves one question remaining."

Jamie cocked an eyebrow. "What else?"

"For the life support blowers, would you like a Pine, Tropical Breeze, or New Starship scent?"

———

The Briefing Room was filled with uniformed officers. The only refreshment: coffee. As the attendees filtered in, all early, it was clear that message had been relayed with sufficient clarity. Their captain was not in a mood to be fucked with.

Up and down both sides of the conference table, all eyes fixed on Jessie. Her opening greeting set the meeting's tone.

"I have been on a comm with my mother."

Even from those who'd never met Amy Ramsey, that declaration drew cringes. From Trebla and Eric, those looks of sympathetic horror doubled. Even Harmony appeared discomfited by proxy.

Once the weight of her pronouncement had had time to settle, Jessie continued. "My father is missing. He has stolen the *Whitechapel*."

Lisa, brave soul that she was, piped up. "Barely counts as a separate incident, now, does it? Hardly got done returning it from the last time he nicked it."

Jessie chose not to delve into the nitpicking world of petty legalese. Loaning someone something with no predetermined end to said lending, and with no contractual terms notarized, was as good as a gift. Since the man who'd taught her that was the thief in question, it stood to reason that he'd argue that A) he hadn't stolen it, and B) it was technically in Junior's name, so since he hadn't handed it directly to the registered owner, he was still mid-borrow.

"My mother has not heard from my father regarding his departure. Here's what we know so far. As best Mom knows, Carl was completely unaware of Aunt Jamie still being alive until Eric blurted it out over dinner last night."

"Sorry."

That hangdog look and contrite cowering weren't going to draw Jessie into the trap of letting Eric center this meeting on his own guilt. "Carl convinced the overnight bridge watch to grant him airlock passage around 2355 hours last night. He is not responding to comms, left no itinerary, and has not shown up in any public arrest logs on either side of the Eyndar Empire border."

"Some luck, at any rate," Mindy grumbled.

"He is in possession of the knowledge that Jamie Ramsey is alive, that her ship is named *Scylla*, and that she's gone to ground at a hidden repair base until her ship can defend itself again. Kinniss, you able to shed any light on where to find the *Scylla*?"

"Nope," the plouph replied flippantly. Then again, it was hard to tell with plouph. Their body language and verbal tics weren't as well known as many xeno species Jessie was familiar with.

"Is that a nope you *can't* help or a nope you *won't*?" Jessie pressed. "You're her security chief. You must know where the *Scylla* goes for repairs."

"There's junk only she knows. Captain kicks it, lotta stuff'd change on the *Scylla*, even if Sofia took over for her. Makes sense, though. What if I got captured on a hostile ship? Interrogated. Tortured. Maybe they'd use magic, even."

Kinniss cast a glance at the wizardly contingent at the table. Charlotte looked as in-place with her uniform on as Eric looked out of place in his. Hadrian sported a new look, and it was hard to say whether Jessie approved. Little about the jet-black robes said "military" except for perhaps the square shoulders that lent him at least a modicum of dignity as he slouched away a full two centimeters' height seated alongside his brethren.

"How could I protect those secrets, then?" Kinniss continued.

"Fine. If I find out later you knew how to contact Jamie and wouldn't tell us, I'll deal with you myself. As for the rest of you, we're mounting a search. We need to find, contact, or collect my father and get him out of eyndar space before he gets his stupid ass killed. If he'd have ever been safe wandering the slime zone of the galaxy, those days are somewhere back in his ion trail."

Trebla raised a hand. Jessie pointed and nodded like this was some kind of classroom.

"What if we track Uncle Carl halfway around the galaxy, run smack into your Aunt Jamie, and he's already found her?"

Hadrian gave a harrumph but didn't comment when Jessie shot him a glare.

"We'll ship him off to New Garrelon to let my mother deal with him."

There were grumbles of agreement around the Briefing Room that this seemed like a just punishment.

"In the meantime, we're going to work off the assumption that Carl Ramsey is out on his own, vulnerable, blundering around, and bound to get himself into lethal trouble if we don't get to him first. That said, we don't know where he went. The Eyndar Empire is larger than ARGO ever was, and more sparsely colonized. A methodical search is out of the question. We need leads. We need clues. We need out-of-orbit thinking to counter an out-of-orbit thinker.

"And maybe we might need a little magic."

Hadrian nodded solemnly. "I'll zip us to. I'll zip us fro. I'll drop us where we need to go."

Jessie pointed past him. "Great, but I was thinking of her."

"Me?" Sparta inquired. "I was startled to receive an invitation. I didn't think these sorts of affairs involved a plus-one, but what do I know about military etiquette?"

"No. You were invited on your own merits. Order of Delphi, right? Finders of lost keys and missing dogs, even if no one wants you telling their fortunes; am I right?"

"You're aren't *wrong*, but neither are you correct. Your assumption that I may discover the location of your father—whom I've known only briefly—over the span of a larger significant swath of the galaxy is... endearingly optimistic." She turned to Hadrian. "Do you know if the pea thing is common among technologists?"

"I wouldn't think so," Hadrian replied.

"What's the pea thing?" Jessie asked of Sparta. Before the oracle could have hoped to answer, she repeated the question, directed at Eric. "What's the pea thing? Do you know any 'pea thing'?"

Eric gulped. "Um..."

"Take a boat. A regular old floating bucket on a terrestrial lake or pond," Sparta lectured. Someone had mentioned her working as a teaching assistant at Oxford, and Jessie could hear that in her voice. "Row, paddle, or science your way across. Somewhere along the journey, a companion in the boat drops a single pea—"

"Frozen or fresh-picked?" Eric asked.

"Doesn't matter."

"It does! A frozen pea floats!!"

"Let's use a pebble, then," Sparta said brusquely. "A companion jettisons a pebble over the side of the boat somewhere along the way. At the end of the trip, they ask if you'll find it for them."

"They can fuck right off," Jessie replied without a moment's hesitation.

Sparta sighed. "The size comparison differs by mind-boggling orders of magnitude. The actual pea test is a rudimentary assessment of divination magic. A skilled oracle *can* find that pea in some random little pond. I did mine in a decorative pond near my parents' house on Earth. Drop that same pea in the Pacific Ocean, and I daresay it's gone for good."

"Fish would get it," Eric reasoned.

"Fish had better *not* get Dad," Jessie shot back. She turned her attention back to their visiting oracle. "Fine. It's a tall order. But it's still an order. You want free room and board, you earn your keep."

Sparta had this annoying regal look in her eyes. "Quite reasonable, and you'll get my best efforts, though I'd have been remiss not to forewarn you of its futility."

"As for the rest of you," Jessie continued. "Mindy. Trebla.

Newsfeeds. Police scans. Anything you can find that might hint at a nosy human poking at business that's not his. Check both sides of the border, just in case. Arrest reports. Disturbances. My father has a nostalgic thing for dive bars."

"On it," Trebla confirmed.

"Count on us," Mindy added.

"Uom'pe. Makket. We're going to pause our little charade that you two were legitimate business people. I need your underworld connections. Try to find the *Scylla*. If we can get on the trail, we're likely to run across my father. And if any of his detective work earns him a price on his head, sign up to collect it."

"Very…"

"Ceasing-charade-immediately-If-you'll-excuse-me-prematurely-from-the-remainder-of-this-briefing-I'll-get-started-at-once."

"… well."

"Hang in here. I'm almost done. Lisa, I want you tracking down the *Whitechapel*. It's your ship. If you've got any special insights, tricks, or ways to locate it, now's the time to pull them out."

Lisa scowled. "Din't never expect it to be Carl who nicked it. I mean. Yeah. He did once already. But that don't hardly count."

"Grosstet, I know you've mostly retired to a leisurely life of holovids and beer—"

"CULTURE EDUCATION AND NECESSARY REFRESHMENT…"

"But can you dig into the *Arete* scanner logs and see if there's anything we're missing because us non-haathee are still guessing at how some of your stuff works?"

"I SHALL DO SO. HOWEVER, I DO WONDER WHETHER AN ELDER OF YOUR SPECIES IS TRULY

IN SUCH DANGER MERELY FROM LAUNCHING AN INVESTIGATION."

"My kind hates being investigated," Jessie explained. "The eyndar have that in common. Carl is going to be making a lot of people nervous if he starts checking into a rogue starship operated by a human in eyndar space. And nervous outlaws tend to kill their problems."

"NO MATTER HOW MANY HOLOVIDS I VIEW, THE QUARRELSOME NATURE OF YOUR SPECIES CONTINUES TO AMAZE ME."

"Any questions?" Jessie asked, not allowing *anything* to divert her off course. They all had questions. They had them by the millions. But none were for Jessie. After an appropriate and awkward wait, she nodded. "Dismissed."

The next morning, Mindy showed up at her regular maintenance appointment in Med Bay with drooping eyes and a fresh cup of coffee she'd be allowed to drink once her systems reports were complete.

"Good morning," Dr. Richelieu greeted her with a degree of chipperness Mindy couldn't even fake in return. "I've avoided checking your remote readings in advance of your checkup, but your face is a spoiler for neuro-response time metrics."

Mindy grunted and shambled toward the examination table.

Dr. Richelieu paused. A look of concern wrinkled that Hollyworld face. "Could I get a verbal greeting? If something's gone wrong in the language center of—"

"I'm fine. Just exhausted is all. Didn't set no alarm for beddy-bye time. Slogged them newsfeeds and copper-rags till 'bout maybe two hours ago. Daph nods off here and there on the regular. Hard to think anyfing of it. She wakes up from one, look me up and down. Asks if I know what time it is."

"Did you?"

"Fuck me if every bloody newsfeed don't have its time stamped all over the rotten place. I know it's a dusty sack of words, but 'time lost all meaning' sort of... happened."

"Well, we're going to get you up on the monitors and see what's going on in there." The doctor rapped a knuckle on Mindy's skull. It didn't hurt her physically, but her pride took a dent from the level of condescension.

Mindy tried peeking at the handheld scanner in Dr. Richelieu's hand or glancing back at the computer screens behind her. She gleaned no insight before the answers were revealed to her.

"Go ahead and have your coffee," the doctor told her. "You clearly need the boost. I hope it was worth it."

"Depends. What's it worth ruling out a hundred planets maybe-kinda-sort of? You got the faintest notion what kind of shite gray-haired, pale, cocky, spacer sons-of-bitches get up to out in the galaxy?"

"The faintest," Dr. Richelieu agreed with a hint of a smile. "I wasn't going to say anything in the briefing yesterday, but I doubt Jessie and Eric's father is going to need saving. He's a cagey old veteran outlaw. We're more likely to find him in a morgue than wandering the streets of a border colony. And he's more likely to contact us from aboard the *Scylla* than either of those."

Mindy sipped her drink. The shock of the heat pouring down her throat felt good. Soon, the caffeine would kick in. "Be nice of the bloke to up and put in a comm to the captain and let us all off the hook."

"That's the thing. I've heard plenty of stories. I wouldn't

say I know him well, personally, but my mother flew with Carl Ramsey's crew for a while when she was young."

"Which—?"

"Esper," Harmony interrupted the question snippily before composing herself quickly. "From all I've heard of those old days, he's a master of avoiding responsibility. He's no fool, as much as he acts like one. Carl Ramsey will be aware that his sister doesn't want to be found and that Jessie won't want him looking. So he'll go *out* of his way to not let either of them get *in* the way of what *he* wants to do."

Mindy snickered.

"Something funny?"

"Don't that sort of remind you of anyone? How many of us is doing anything but what we bloody please? Present chores aside, mind you..."

Dr. Richelieu shut down her datapad and pushed her hair back with her goggles. "Point taken. Do you mind a somewhat frank discussion of a side topic?"

Mindy squirmed inwardly. Who was she to argue with the doc? "All right."

"You and Lt. Morgan have been close for some time now."

"Guess so. Not like we's counting days or nothing."

The doctor took a seat beside Mindy on the examination table. "Have the two of you ever considered starting a family?"

A nervous chuckle escaped Mindy. "Look, anything were to happen to you, I'm sure as we'd take great care of Xrista until we got her to your folks. I mean, if we can convince Uom'pe to give her up. Old turtle dotes on the nipper like she hatched Xrista from her own egg."

"That's nice to hear, but that's not what I was getting at. I know you're young. You've got a long life ahead of you. Technology permitting, Lt. Morgan might, too. But while the calendar says you're older than her, she's watching the end of her prime fertile years racing toward her."

"She... mention this to you?"

"Look, I know it's invasive, but I see a lot more when I read your scans than just whether or not the muscular and neural enhancements are performing optimally. In checking for side effects and overall health, I learn a lot of incidental facts about all my patients. Frankly, that goes for everyone aboard except the wizards. Certain facts of overall biological health just state the obvious when you look at the data."

"Facts? What kind of facts?"

"I can tell the difference between lust, infatuation, and love."

Mindy felt her face warm. "Um... does that mean she...?"

"Oh, for goodness' sake. Yes. The two of you are dopey about it—that's the medical term," Dr. Richelieu joked. "Now, I know that the wider galaxy isn't all that welcoming of mixed-species couples, but there are some options if you two do decide to raise a family together."

"I mean. I suppose plenty of tykes come through here. Orphans and whatnot. You sayin' to just pick one out?" Mindy paused briefly. "Not sure how I'd feel about that."

"No. I mean a biological child from the two of you."

Mindy's mind went blank.

It was easy to forget, here and there, that this haathee medicine bordered on witchcraft. Or that her personal doc was a bigwig from Harmony Goddamn Bay. All these checkups and the blasé treatment of the nano-drones in her blood made deadlifting 150 kilos and learning Jiara in five days seem normal.

But this...

"You serious? That even possible?"

"Yes."

Mindy blew a breath to clear her mind. "Wow. This H-tech ain't fooling around."

"Oh. It's not anything to do with haathee technology. It's one of those Harmony Bay projects that didn't really leave the research phase. Not exactly the sort of thing you can set up trials for. Imagine trying to advertise for participants and it getting onto the newsfeeds that Harmony Bay is encouraging species mixing. Our stock would have gone into negative numbers. There would have been protests."

"But... you can do it?"

"It's really not that different from how Xrista was born."

Mindy looked over. Harmony stared expectantly. She invited the question. "What do you mean? She half some other species? You never say nothing about her father. None of us ask."

"She's human. Just human."

"So, her father...?"

Dr. Richelieu shook her head. "No father."

"You mentioned that your sisters are—"

"No second mother."

"Then..."

Harmony put a hand on Mindy's shoulders. "I've gained access to the galaxy's most advanced genetics recombination technology. I could recreate my younger sisters with ease. Xrista was trivial by comparison. So is... her future sister."

Mindy's gaze strayed downward. "You're preggers?"

Dr. Richelieu slid off the table and headed out of the examination room. Curiosity burning, Mindy quickly followed. In her office, the doctor approached a spot on the wall.

Mindy's heart froze.

"What? It's not as if you left traces of your DNA on the panel and inside when you snuck a peek. I'd rather you knew than guessed or dug around investigating on your own out of curiosity."

The panel slid out with a touch. Inside, the strange glass chamber wafted a fog of cool steam. Mindy joined her. The embryo floated there, not a dream as she might have put out of her mind, but real and at the fore of this conversation.

"I've never been pregnant," Dr. Richelieu explained. "I took a sabbatical for a few months leading up to her birth. Only a couple of my assistants know. You hear parents say their child is such a delight, they wouldn't mind another just like them. Well, circumstances of upbringing aside, this little girl will be."

Mindy pointed to the inscription on the side of the chamber. "H3. Does that mean...?"

"It means I haven't decided on a name yet. Harmony 3 is a placeholder."

"So when you tell everyone Xrista don't have a father, that's just you being cheeky, now, innit?"

Dr. Richelieu shrugged. "Yeah. It's a canned answer that shuts most people up about it."

"Does that mean she's not really—?" The doctor's raised finger stopped her mid-sentence.

"Xrista is a person. She's real. I'm her mother, legally and socially. Biologically, she's a twin sister born thirty years later. It was actually easier than the technology that allowed my mothers to combine their DNA to give birth to my younger sisters. That tech is all over Martian and Earthling space now. Expensive, sure, but getting more affordable as it becomes less exotic."

"Not as exotic as that other thing..."

"A little girl of your own," the doctor offered. "A mix of azrin and human. I can manipulate the gene expression so she looks entirely like either species, but you'll each see enough of yourselves in her to know she's both of yours."

"You sure it'd be a girl?"

"Neither of you possesses a Y chromosome. I can't work around that yet. Not without a third donor, at least. If that was important to you, I could—"

"Given me enough to think on." Mindy rested a hand on her abdomen. "Never really seriously considered being a mother."

"Daphne has."

Mindy looked up suddenly. "She told you?"

"She asked me to talk to you. This was her idea." The doctor smirked. "That enhanced cross-linking in her brain. So... I'll answer any questions, medical, moral, or maternal. I don't need an answer right now or even ever. The option isn't going away; there's no time limit. Though in full disclosure, Daphne doesn't have a lot of her reproductive prime left. But if you choose to carry the child, you've got decades ahead of you where there would essentially be zero risk."

"Oi..."

"It's a lot to think about. I know. But when I see you killing yourselves looking for Carl Ramsey, I just know that there are aspiring parents out there in the galaxy waiting for a chance to do better than that.

"Be the kind of moms that don't send your kids scouring the galaxy to look for you because you're an idiot. OK?"

"That much, I can guarantee."

Mindy left Med Bay in a daze, and it took four comms reminding her before she got back to work sifting the omni for clues.

━━

Hadrian strolled the vast, empty corridors of the starship *Arete*. For all that it was built by alien hands, it didn't feel so weird or unwelcoming as a typical Boston shopping plaza. If this was going to be his home to defend, however long he chose to remain, he felt that he ought to know his way around. The little pictures they showed him failed to do the spacefaring boat justice.

It was also nice spending some time separate from Sparta. They got along well, and he liked the idea of keeping it that way. He hadn't asked where she was going. Hadrian had his guesses, but they were just that. An agreement to meet for dinner at the ship's communal dining lounge would be their next planned encounter.

Starship travel relaxed him.

This specimen was too large by far to pretend anything about coziness. But the crew was an interesting tableau, if not a family. And there were few enough of them that he'd learn all their names in short order—at least, if enough of the ratatoret came out to meet him.

Sneakers came and went. Despite an upgrade to a semi-official uniform, he'd refused new footwear. A stop at a campus-adjacent sporting goods store and a hundred or so terras had gained him this pair, and it had been with Hadrian since his first week in this body. The corridors of the *Arete* would have their chance to wear down the soles until he truly *needed* another.

He peeked in open doors and paused at intersections to study haathee art installations. Until someone tried to board the vessel or go very fast with it, learning his way around the place *was* work, by thunder.

Pelting footsteps alerted him of company long before it arrived. Short of an ambush, Hadrian didn't worry at the coming of anyone, and this pursuer wasn't anyone he'd ever worried about for his own safety.

"Hadrian!"

He turned and waited, hands in his sleeves and a blank expression on his face. "What is it, Wizard Eric?"

Eric Ramsey drew up short, panting for breath, resting his hands on his knees. "There's no one. Around here. I have to. Know."

"There's nothing so urgent that you can't catch your breath first."

"Right," Eric replied, then huffed until he was able to stand upright. "It's just you and me here."

"If you're looking for a rematch, I'll just—"

"You're him. Right?"

"I'm me. Yes."

"I knew it! I knew you were you! I didn't dare tell anyone because I wasn't sure, and then—"

He cut off as there was no air entering or exiting his lungs. "Stop."

Eric nodded hastily, and Hadrian loosened up the air around him. It was a trick he'd come up with years ago. Collapsing a wizard's lungs was a lot more taxing than simply turning the air in their immediate vicinity as thick as a sponge.

"I won't tell anyone."

"We're alone, like you said. Won't tell anyone *what?*"

"That you were Enzio Stiles and Khosrau and Mordecai The Brown."

"Ah."

"You are. Aren't you? I'm not wrong."

Hadrian nodded slowly. "And, if you didn't think you could keep that secret, you know how to hide that knowledge from yourself. Right?"

"I could, but—I mean, I think I've done all right up until now."

"Who have you told?"

"Jessie. I mean, when you were Khosrau and Enzio was dead and Mom and Dad told us about Nancy, I had a theory."

"Did she believe you?"

"Um. You'd have to ask *her*."

Hadrian took that as a "no." He knew the Ramsey kids well enough to realize that Jessie was unlikely to humor Eric's wild theories. "Who else?"

"Let's see... Nope... Nope... Uh... I think maybe Aunt Tiffany."

"She knows."

Eric blew a sigh. "That's a relief."

"You're not very good with secrets."

"How was I supposed to *know* that Dad wasn't supposed to know that Jamie didn't want him to know she was alive? I mean, who tells me anything?"

"I did. Once."

"Why are you here now? Does Dad know? Does Sparta? What happened to the guy who was Hadrian before you? Is he in Mortania permanently, or—?"

"Your father and Sparta both know. The original Hadrian traded this body and its lack of galactic responsibilities for an empire. He's Khosrau now, and he's welcome to it. As for why I'm here... I decided I wanted to get back to roaming the galaxy. Earth got boring."

"Wow."

"You asked."

"Yep. I sure did." Eric appeared mentally overtaxed. The team of gerbils running around behind his eyeballs had invoked a work stoppage. Hadrian allowed him time to negotiate a return to duty. "So. What do I call you?"

"Boss?" Hadrian suggested with a smirk. "The nincompoop previous resident of this body never got himself even a half-decent nickname. Three syllables is really beyond the pale for daily use."

"Haddy?"

"I will *manually* remove that one from your brain if I have to. Is that understood?"

"Gotcha. No on 'Haddy.'"

"Just call me Hadrian. If a suitable sobriquet comes along, I'll inform you. Otherwise, my name is fine. And I do mean the name this body is known by."

"Dad mentioned you kind of looked like Mort. Is... he right about that?"

"Nothing wrong with that one's eyes. Yeah. Dead ringer, just about. Taller, though. Been stepping down through heights since Enzio, but this skinny weed's built for seeing over crowds."

"Sparta must have had a hard time finding a guy taller than her."

Hadrian harrumphed. "As if that were her primary criteria in finding a partner. Her mind's as sharp as an obsidian blade and filled with mischief. I used to think Nancy was my soulmate, and at the time, maybe she was the right match for me. But I look back and see the pretension, the entitlement, the social climbing."

"Weren't you Mr. Aristocrat on Earth?"

"At the time. Didn't realize until I left for a while just how much I found all the bullshit to be bullshit and how many of them took it completely seriously."

"If you ever want to take another crack at it all, I've been working on some theories to—"

"If your next words will be about time travel, eat them."

Eric froze. Then he gulped.

"They were, then?"

Eric nodded.

"Look here. When I was playing Khosrau, I was mad. I was mad at Nancy for getting on the wrong side of a coup. I was mad at everyone who didn't stop the traitors. I took over from the inside of that coup and I made a lot of people pay for what they'd done. For some, it was belated vengeance of my own, long overdue. For the rest, pure spite. Is that any way to run an empire?"

"No?" Eric ventured.

"Damn right, it's not. Suddenly, I'm the final word on treaties. I've got Mars declaring war on me. The nonhuman ARGO members and protectorates all picked up their blue-green marbles and went home. Senators are plotting against me or angling for my favor. Then, get this, they want heirs. Imperialists feel the need to ensure dynastic stability. Hogwash. I could have ruled forever. But, no. They need drama. They need pageantry. I ended up with a harem so that no single conniving upstart would get the satisfaction of thinking she was second place in the empire."

Eric put a hand on Hadrian's shoulder. "Sounds awful."

"It was!" He huffed. "But now I'm free of all that hullabaloo. Just a magical prodigy running from responsibility. On a lark. With his girl. And we will *not* be resetting the timeline, now, will we?"

Eric shook his head.

"Are you avoiding speaking because you know I can tell when you're lying?"

Eric hesitated before nodding meekly.

"Eric, I'm an octogenarian in a 22-year-old body, so I've little ground to stand on ethically. But if I catch you trying to ruin the life I've built from the ashes of tragedy, I will personally come in there and scoop out every bit of magical knowledge in that head of yours. You think it's too big in there. Too vast. That you could bottle me up and lead me on a merry chase for longer than both our natural lifespans. I am stronger than I've ever been, stronger than you'll ever be, and I'm keeping what's mine. My life. My memories. The actual events that have taken place, good and bad. *Intelligas?*"

Eric nodded.

Hadrian glared.

"Yes."

"Good."

"But what if Dad dies?"

Hadrian's eyes unfocused. "He's too old to be out there on his own. Not as sharp as he used to be. If... if it comes to that, maybe we can discuss shoving a few choice grains of sand back up the hourglass."

There should have been laws against sand. Then again, even if there were, the denizens of *this* colony wouldn't have cared. The very name of the place, Hope Springs, was a rebellion. Most of the surface was covered in water; the rest, in sand. Native lives had never crawled out of the vast mono-ocean, but plenty of shit lived below the surface.

It was as if someone had poured water over an Earth-like until Mt. Everest was the only part poking above the waves, then baked it mercilessly. Carl had looked the place up on the way, just to be prepared. Old treaties had designated the planet for scientific expeditions, and those treaties had been ignored from the start. Solidly in former EADZ territory, it was a trading post that fed itself on stuff that was not entirely unlike fish.

Day and night meant little here. Four visible moons kept the sky a pale sort of bright and the tides chaotic. Carl navigated the streets by feel. His datapad had a map, but he knew better than to check it like a tourist. His memory of that top-down, overhead view didn't match well with the geography anyway. It was enough to make a guy think a rogue colony in unclaimed space didn't draw a lot of cartographers.

After some wandering, Carl and the practice range blaster on his hip entered the open back door of a "fish"-processing factory. Vast undersea pipes vacuumed in sea life, and this place tried to turn it into food. However well they succeeded in that venture, they definitely turned the local wildlife into a putrid odor that pervaded the place.

"You lost, spacer?" someone asked. He wore slime-stained coveralls with rubber gloves and boots but, importantly, no breathing mask.

"Depends. Is Baby Boy here?" As nicknames went, Carl was glad he'd ended up with Blackjack. Going through life as a grown-ass man known as Baby Boy would have been enough to get *him* to move to a colony where no one had heard of him. And the first thing he'd do when he got there *wasn't* to tell everyone.

"Who's asking?" the "fish"-worker demanded.

"Some lost spacer."

The worker grunted and pointed. "Heavy guy with the datapad. Don't waste his time."

Carl didn't need to be told. He wended his way through machines he couldn't identify and avoided puddles even more mysterious in origin.

"You lookin' for me, spacer? You found me," Baby Boy greeted him brusquely.

"Orrey sent me," Carl explained. It was amazing the sorts of things you could win in a poker game. Money was easy. Jewelry, personal electronics, custom blasters... that was all standard stuff. But an intro to a black site repair shop could be had if the cards fell right and the wrong people lost. Knowing the right people could get you far in life. But knowing all the wrong ones worked nearly as well.

"How do I know Orrey's not in lockup somewhere and you're a cop?"

Carl shrugged. "I'm open to suggestions."

Usually, playing it this casual kept things from proceeding to the point of proof. To his credit, Baby Boy was a cautious cat. He scratched his head with a corner of his datapad before declaring, "All right. Follow me."

They headed up a flight of grated metal stairs that rang with the impact of each boot and into an office just big enough for a quiet meeting, though with its big glass windows, not a private one.

Baby Boy settled in at the desk and hit an intercomm button. "Send in Tazzle."

A moment later, a skinny bald guy poked his head in. "Boss?"

"You were short last week."

Tazzle drew back, shocked. "C'mon. You said it would slide."

"Yeah. Well. Changed my mind. You been sliding too much lately." Baby Boy reached under his desk and drew a blaster. Kason-40 by the look of it, old enough to have a pension of its own. The "fishery" boss pushed it across the desk toward Carl. "Put two in his kneecaps."

Never one to refuse a free blaster, Carl picked up the weapon he was offered. Frankly, heading in here, he'd suspected he was being set up to kill someone. "I'm pretty sure some Earth Interstellar spook would kneecap a guy if he had to," he told Baby Boy as he took careful aim.

"Boss, boss, you don't gotta—"

"Fine. Put a hole in his skull, then," Baby Boy snapped.

Amateur hour. Fucking amateur hour.

Carl flicked a switch. "Nice try. You had the safety on. I've seen plenty of safety blackouts in my time. Never trust a lack of an indicator light." He raised the barrel toward Tazzle's skull.

Neither man appeared as if they could move as fast as they did next. Tazzle collapsed to the floor and curled into a fetal position. Baby Boy knocked the desk askew in his haste to wrest the weapon from Carl's hand.

He allowed the weapon to be taken away without resistance, then patted his own as the panic in the room subsided. "I've disabled the safety on every blaster I've ever owned."

"Good way to shoot your dick off," Tazzle muttered as he got to his feet.

"Hair triggers are for wimps with no grip and posers who think it makes them sound like they're a temper tantrum from mass murder. I was with the Ruckers back when they were something. Never knew a syndicate guy who kept a hair trigger. Safety off. Always. And enough pull on the trigger that it won't misfire in the buffet line. Now, we gonna talk starships or have we all wasted our time here?"

"What do you need?"

"I'm semi-retired," Carl explained. "Helping out an old friend. Got a ship—let's call it 165 m—looking for some low-profile repairs. Heard you can take on something that size."

"Is it seaworthy?"

"We're willing to pay to pump out any seawater that gets in. How soon can you take us?"

Baby Boy sized Carl up. There wasn't a need for any extraneous Carls this time. The base unit was perfect for this kind of shit.

"Got an opening right now. How soon can you have the ship here?"

Damn. The Hope Springs pirate shipyard was a one-bay

operation. If he had a spot available in his schedule, that meant that the *Scylla* wasn't here.

"I'll contact my captain. Should be able to get here in two to three days."

"There's a holding fee…"

Carl nodded. "Understood. But I'm off comms and not carrying the payment. We'll have to take our chances. Someone cuts ahead of us, we'll wait our turn."

No one hassled Carl on his way out. He'd passed their test. Until he no-showed with his mystery client, Baby Boy and his minions would see Carl as a walking promise of terras—but only if he lived.

Mysteriously, no one at the landing yard bothered him either, not even for a parking fee.

That explicable turn of manufactured good fortune didn't solve Carl's larger problem, however. He was running out of options at the edge of the Eyndar Empire. He was going to have to start looking inside eyndar space.

━━━

Empty space aplenty found itself aboard the starship *Arete*. A fortuitous name. A fortuitous vessel. A sacred charge, bound in blood. Well, not *Sparta's* blood, but the captain's ties of family certainly carried a weight of duty and honor that couldn't be ignored.

Not that she expected anything to come of her efforts.

Hadrian had doted on her with enchanted jewelry, but he understood her craft so poorly. Rather than aid in her efforts at revealing the unknown, she actually found them more useful in suppressing her instinctive and intrusive divinations.

Sparta found herself a refuge in a forgotten intersection deep within the *Arete's* bowels. Several had offered their services, but each also had its own distinctive aura. The natural beauty of an alien world. The interplay of animals in an ecosystem. One with art depicting exotic acts of lovemaking only possible with a prehensile trunk spoke to her personally. But this wasn't a task for herself.

Her chosen haven was a spiral of community. From even a mere pictograph, she understood the philosophy conveyed. The wide, diverse haathee species was one herd. Inward, clockwise, back in time, and it came to the center, the self. But surrounding that self was the family unit.

Sparta crossed her legs at the very center of the floor's mosaic depiction, composed of colored metal tiles in a myriad of shapes.

Her jewels, bless Hadrian, would only impede her. She'd brought along a small coffer, shielded against magical influences. Laying the coffer open on the floor, one by one she undid clasps and wiggled loose backings, placing each chain and ring and stud inside.

Her mind tingled. It was a sensation she'd suppressed naturally before meeting Hadrian, but with his gifts, she'd learned to rely on their help. Free of those impediments, her natural divination crawled free of her control.

The empty chamber at an intersection of corridors sprang to ghostly life with the afterimages of haathee.

Most passed through the chamber. Some carried strange objects or beverages. Others strolled in mixed pairs. Those who lingered reclined and snacked or petted one another with those trunks of theirs. She learned more of this species in a few breathless moments of wonder than she had in her chats with the vessel's owner.

Like muscle trained against a burdensome weight, her strength had grown. Now free, her mind expanded.

Closing her eyes, a vertigo overtook her. The spirits swirled away as Sparta clenched and focused. Serenity was the tool of the spirit-deaf, calming the mind to hear the faintest whisper. Sparta instead fought against a cacophony, listening for a singular voice in a maelstrom choir.

Time and thought snapped apart, no longer on speaking terms. Yesterday and tomorrow blended into today. With eyes squeezed so tightly shut that a headache brewed behind them, Wizard Sparta reached blindly into the small bag she'd tucked into her belt. Inside, her fingers closed around a bar rag.

According to one of the adorable tavernkeepers in the ship's saloon, this scrap of cloth had been kept in reserve for the watering hole's founder. As personal possessions went, it was a paltry thing. Normally, when searching for a lost loved one, an oracle would request something with a spiritual connection. A ring. A trophy. A childhood toy—all the more effective when the missing person *was* a child.

But Carl Ramsey stomped through life rather than tiptoed. His spiritual footprints left a trail a star-drive mechanic could follow. Sparta could scarcely imagine the work it had taken Hadrian—Mordecai, at the time, or Enzio—to sweep up those footprints everywhere they went together.

Sparta's perception raced across the Black Ocean, pulled by instinct, reeled in by fate.

At a derelict space station, the perception halted. Visions overlapped. Non sequitur events jumbled.

Eyndar in the vision speak their own language, a gibberish of snarls and yips and growls and howls.

An escape pod tumbles through the void.

The *Whitechapel.* Open ramp. Carl exiting.

A different hangar, the same style but with different ships within. Two laaku and Carl strike some kind of bargain, sealed with a handshake.

In a crowded bar, a dozen species mix, some Sparta hadn't

seen in person. Carl slips into a booth with two azrin and a plouph.

A starship explodes.

Quick flashes. Eyndar conferring. Different pairs, but always one face familiar from the previous vision. Amid the gibbering, one word stands out. Over and over.

Blackjack.

Blackjack.

Blackjack.

Blackjack.

A scream tears through the vision. It's Jessie Ramsey's voice. "NOOOOOOOOOOOOO!"

The vision breaks apart.

Sparta wobbled and put a hand to the floor to keep from toppling even from a seated position.

Haathee spirits looked on, concerned, as if able to perceive her. Sparta waved them off.

Pawing around amid waves of dizziness, she found the coffer and clumsily donned pieces of jewelry. It took her nose chain and two earrings before the spirits faded and her mind cleared.

She remembered everything, but it was a jumble. All that mattered was: she needed to find Jessie and relay what she'd learned as quickly as possible.

Lurching to her feet, Sparta felt her breakfast making a return trip. She left it splattered on the tile mosaic, blotting out a father figure.

⊏⊐

Up.

Down.

Up.

Down.

190 kilos rose with each press of the bar away from Jessie Ramsey's chest. Ten more than yesterday. Twenty more than last week. Double what she'd ever trained with prior to the H-tech infusion of her muscles.

The drones fired individual fibers, ensuring full and efficient use of each muscle, tearing tissue so that it would grow back even stronger. Except that with each generation of cells, the blueprint evolved.

Even as she'd grown stronger, Jessie's physique had slimmed down. She'd gained 5 kilos but gone down a full uniform size. She was getting denser, more compact. Her bones were taking on extra mineral content, forming microstructures like a bio-graphene honeycomb.

She poured sweat.

Between sets, she drained bottle after bottle of a syrupy concoction packed with nutrients and electrolytes, not to mention the preferred replication materials for the drone factories. The stuff tasted awful, but she'd stopped tasting it at all. The gunk had coated her tongue and rendered the tastebuds there inoperable.

The worst part of her plan to find Carl had been her own superfluousness in it.

Once they had a lead, she'd go planetside, knock some skulls together, get answers. She'd been *trained* for shit like that. But she'd never been in intelligence other than her brief, disastrous stint on Phabian. Cultivating leads, vacuuming the nebulae—so to speak—for leads, maintaining a network of contacts. All that stuff was social, when her specialty had been the antisocial.

Britney wandered in, a towel over her shoulders and a pint-sized duffel clenched in one fist. "Afternoon, Captain."

Jessie gave a nod, still not fully caught up with her breath. "Medic."

"Need a spot with those free weights? Wouldn't want the comm that you crushed your skull under a bar."

Suspicion crept in. "Did Harmony send you to spy on me?"

The easy chuckle before her reply disarmed Jessie. "No. I just have my own training to get in." She nodded to the bottle in Jessie's hand. "Stuff sure does taste like last week's yogurt, huh?"

"You've tried it?"

Britney unzipped her duffel and pulled out an unopened bottle of her own. "Doc started me up on the stuff soon as I got my own drones."

"You too? How many people is Harmony augmenting?"

"As many as ask? I don't have a number. If that's an official request, I can head over to Med Bay and—"

Jessie waved her off as Britney was backing toward the gym's exit. "No. Nothing official. And sure. We can trade off."

To Jessie's shock, Britney picked up a pair of 25 kg plates and added one to either end of the bar. "There we go. I'll do the swaps. Not *your* fault I wandered in on your workout."

"Are you sure about that?" Jessie asked dubiously as the medic settled onto her back beneath the bar.

"Oh, sure. Barely more than I used to use in the corps. Went a bit soft for a while when I got off the pills, but I worked my way back up to something. Dr. Richelieu says—"

"CAPTAIN!" Daphne stormed into the gym, datapad in hand.

"What is it?" Jessie demanded, distracted by watching the bar pumping up and down like a piston as it flexed with each repetition.

Daphne handed the datapad to the captain and firmly shoved her out of the way. "No time for that." Then, she confiscated the bar and settled it onto the cradle like it weighed nothing. "Read."

Jessie's eyes scanned the report.

Hope Springs Colony.

Ship matching the description of the *Whitechapel*.

Pilot was a human male with gray hair and spacer-pale complexion.

Spent less than two hours on the colony.

"This isn't a lot to go on."

Daphne took the datapad back. "I've been doing parallel research on possible locations of hidden pirate shipyards and black-market resupply depots. If I worked for Earth Interstellar, I'd be getting warrants for half a dozen star systems by now. Hope Springs is a mostly aquatic planet. There are enough rumors about an undersea starship repair yard that it would be worth mounting a search there."

"And the info on a mysterious male spacer?"

"Info like that is available on barter. Don't ask what I traded." She lowered her voice and added, "Please."

Jessie could well imagine. But as long as it wasn't anything related to their current whereabouts or secrets of H-tech, she could indulge the request. "How well armed is this Hope Springs place?"

"They have an underdeveloped construction industry."

"I don't see how that's—"

"They lack enough bricks to shit if we show up in orbit."

Jessie smiled. "Nice. Well, if that's our only lead, I suppose we can—"

"CAPTAIN!" This time, the interloper was Wizard Sparta. She burst in, disheveled. She'd misplaced half her piercings. Her hair was discolored with sweat. One side of the tunic/toga thing she wore had fallen off her shoulder. And if

Jessie had any expertise on the subject, that garment was flecked with vomit.

Without knowing any other way to inquire, Jessie went with the most basic, a bewildered "What?"

"I had a vision."

"Looks like it was a doozy," Britney commented.

"A space station in eyndar territory. Cosmopolitan. Your father met with some laaku. I think maybe to book passage after his ship was surrounded by eyndar authorities. Or maybe he will meet with them but hasn't yet."

"I thought you couldn't see the future," Jessie pointed out, annoyed and disturbed at once.

"Can't. Shouldn't. Won't. Can't help but. It's all the same. Tour a museum when the paintings are all falling confetti. Tomorrow's newspaper looks just like today's when you can't see the date."

Daphne's fur bristled. "Even on Earth, no one but wizards looks at a newspaper."

"What station?" Jessie interrupted before the gym conference took a turn for the irrelevant. "Do you have a name?"

"If I heard one, I didn't recognize it. I don't speak eyndar."

"Maybe Charlotte could help," Daphne suggested. "She's good with memories."

"It's not a memory," Sparta snapped. "It was a glimpse."

"It's a memory to you. Now." Jessie was growing frustrated. Perhaps it had been a mistake insisting Hadrian's plus-one participate in the efforts to find Carl.

Sparta pinched the bridge of her nose. "I'd sooner let Hadrian look. It may not be his area of specialty, but at least I trust him. I did hear something, though."

"From my father and those laaku?" Jessie tried to recall details from the blurted gibberish. Uncle Enzio had warned her about oracles. Most of them were harmless, but the extremes numbered among the galaxy's best con men *and* true diviners.

"No. The eyndar. They must not have a name for it in their language because they kept going on and on about a card game."

The blood drained from Jessie's face. "What card game?"

"Blackjack."

———

With the oracle cooped up, trying to get Hadrian to weasel the details of a mystery vision out of her brain, Jessie found herself riding down to the scant surface of a bleak ocean wasteland. Grosstet had the controls of his own shuttle. Despite numerous objections on various grounds, Jessie was done fucking around. Maybe if word got back to Carl about how reckless and bold she was acting in this matter, he might at least drop a comm to let everyone know he was all right.

"THIS IS EXCITING. IS IT NOT?" the haathee pilot asked.

Jessie wanted to deny it. She wanted to claim that excitement was the last thing on her mind, but it was hard to lie that it wasn't in there somewhere. "Yeah. But we're here on a mission. If the human that flounced on and off this colony yesterday *was* my father, then we're going to see the guy he met with."

The fish factory had no official landing zone on its roof, but there was a door for getting up there to maintain the various vents and blowers grumbling away atop the structure. Grosstet set them down not far from it.

"Let's make this quick. We're not here to play nice."

"QUICK. NOT NICE. I HAVE RECEIVED THE MESSAGE."

Jessie hopped down to find the door swinging open with armed resistance already.

"Who do you think you are? Get that fucking thing off the..."

Two guys with blasters pulled up short. They were all gung-ho and full of piss when Jessie showed up on the ramp, coming down at them with a blaster rifle in her hands. When they saw Grosstet in person, they just malfunctioned.

"Where's your boss?" Jessie demanded.

When neither of the pair answered immediately, Grosstet stepped past her. He held his antimatter pistol off to one side. "THIS WEAPON IS TOO MUCH. IF YOU FAIL TO ANSWER, I WILL HURL YOU BODILY FROM THE BUILDING." To prove his threat wasn't idle, he wrapped his trunk around a vent pipe, ripped it from the bolts holding it to the roof, and discarded it like a used drinking straw.

Time to play good cop.

"Look, you take us to your boss and maybe you live to the end of your shift. Don't, and I guarantee you'll be clocking out early today."

All right. Maybe two bad cops could work, too.

"Yeah-yeah. Sure. Gotcha. All bonzer here," the first to rouse himself to usefulness babbled.

The second of the pair panicked. A bolt of plasma flew.

Given that she'd worn a personal shield with an H-tech power source, the odds of the attack having any effect were just about nil. Nevertheless, instincts kicked in. Jessie twisted aside.

Instantly, her muscles spasmed. She doubled over. The protective shield flickered. Red plasma passed clean through it.

"GAH!"

"JESSICA!" Grosstet exclaimed. The haathee strode over, footsteps earthquaking the rooftop, and hurled the gunman through the air. Two more wild, spasmodic blasts sailed errantly as the man's scream followed the arc of his doomed body over the five-story structure's ledge.

"I'm all right," Jessie grunted through the pain. "Just a scorch. Let's get this over with."

"I-I-I-didn't do anything," the dead man's companion protested.

"Take us inside."

Grosstet barely fit. Jessie could barely walk. Their guide was barely retaining the contents of his bladder as they made their way through a mass of catwalks past overhead gantries and pumping controls. The stench, noticeable from up top, trebled in intensity.

"HAVE I MENTIONED THAT I DISLIKE SEA CREATURES?"

"Don't think it's come up."

"THE ONLY THING I APPRECIATE ABOUT THEM IS THE ODOR OF THEIR DEMISE. THIS PLACE SMELLS OF VICTORY."

A fellow the guide called Baby Boy met them outside a shabby industrial office, on a catwalk that bowed under Grosstet's weight.

"You think you can bully *me*? On *my* planet?"

"I think I can snap you in half and show you your own asshole before you die," Jessie snapped back.

Baby Boy glanced up at Grosstet. "Don't know what zoo, lab, or corner of the galaxy you dragged that thing out of, but you just got yourself a bigger stuunji is all. I've got stuunji on my payroll."

Despite her annoyance, Jessie couldn't help but admire this fucker's gumption. She got straight to the point. "You met with someone yesterday. I want to find him."

"I meet with a lot of guys about a lot of stuff. I don't talk about business to anyone whose business it isn't."

"Strange policy for a fishmonger," Jessie challenged. She winced, unable to help herself.

"You might wanna get that looked at. Blaster burns and infections don't go good around all these unfamiliar bacteria we got here."

"THE FISH MAN MAKES A FINE POINT. PERHAPS WE OUGHT TO—"

"I'm *fine*," Jessie snapped. She raised the barrel of her blaster rifle and aimed it at Baby Boy's forehead. "And this guy is going to tell us who he met with and where the guy went, or I'm going to go looking in his brain for myself."

"I run a *legitimate* business," Baby Boy insisted. "My clients prefer anonymity. And if anything happens to me, it'll be bad news for you."

Jessie barked a laugh that made her wound sting anew. "Hah. Do you even know who I am?"

"No one who asks that's ever anyone big."

Oof, even unarmed, the guy had gotten a shot off. "I'm Jessie Ramsey, captain of the *Arete*, the ship that spooked half the orbital traffic of this soggy sweatsock of a planet when we pulled up. Mars Navy checks for backup before so much as hailing us, and I'll be damned if—"

"Did you say Ramsey? Like, as in Blackjack Ramsey?"

"So you *did* see him!"

"WAIT! That motherfucker in here yapping about a no-name ship was Blackjack?"

Never taking both hands off her weapon, Jessie accessed her TeleJack, bringing up an old holo. "This the guy?"

"He was in rougher shape than that, but yeah. That your old man or something? I don't like getting in the middle of family stuff. Had me thinking he was with the Ruckers."

"Believe me, you'd be luckier if he was."

While she had the TeleJack open, a message came in. *"Captain, do you read. Can you respond, Captain?"*

"This had better be important," Jessie warned as she backed away, aware that Baby Boy had an unknown number of armed guards and goons lurking nearby, ready to pounce on any sign of weakness. Mindy knew Jessie wasn't in the mood for games, and her criteria for breaking comm silence had been clear.

"Feed out of the eyndar side. Someone nabbed him."

That counted.

"You're off the hook, fisherman," Jessie informed Baby Boy before lowering her blaster rifle. "I won't bother telling you to keep *my* visit quiet. C'mon, Grosstet, let's head back. I'll grab details on the way."

The chase was on. Someone had found Carl. And with any luck, they'd take a bribe.

"Ain't gonna be me what tells her. You do it."

"I have no desire to be the one who breaks the news. You were already on the comm with her. She'll be expecting it from you."

Mindy and Daphne squared off. Ensign Galapap kept his head down and his feet planted on the console at the helm, staying clear of the fray.

"I got me in command now. I've got seniority. And I say you take the comm when Captain Ramsey rings us up from the shuttle."

The *Arete* was perfectly safe. Orbital space around Hope Springs Colony didn't have any vessels, official or otherwise, that would threaten them. Frankly, the odds that anything had the firepower to put a dent in Grosstet's shuttle were slim.

The occupants of the *Arete*... less than safe. Their captain had a temper.

Daphne whipped an outstretched claw at the comms duty station. "I'll pull Commander Webber out of a session to have her give the order if I have to."

Mindy feigned a cough—badly. "Uh oh, looks like I gotta get meself down to Med Bay."

"I don't think that Dr. Richelieu will—"

"*Shuttle 1 to Bridge,*" Captain Ramsey blared over the comm. "*Where's our sighting and how soon can we be there?*"

The standoff grew tense. Neither party followed through with threats to involve senior officers not present.

"*Shuttle 1 to Bridge. Lt. Sedgwick, do you copy?*"

Daphne backed away from her post, paws up. It wasn't her name that the captain had called out.

Mindy finished a snarl of frustration and cleared the pique from her voice before settling in at comms to answer. "Yeah, Captain. We got ya. It's just... this ain't a pack-and-go sort of intel report."

"*I don't care. We can head to the sighting, deal with shit when we get there. Just be ready to move out.*"

Mindy felt the panic rising. She'd be lucky if Dr. Richelieu wasn't already in a run to scan her for heart failure the way her pulse was racing. "Yeah. Right. Good on ya. Definitely can do that. Little place called Trade Gate 4."

"*Four? That's an awfully low number. Must be close to their core.*"

"It's core all right," Mindy confirmed. "Trade Gate. Means they let xenos like humans roam free. Also means security's tighter than a haathee handshake."

A little background toot of amusement broke the mood, but not for long.

"*I'll pull schematics as soon as we get back. This may be*

more of a hostage standoff than a jailbreak. And be ready to chase down any ship they send to move him as cargo."

"Cargo? Captain, you ain't gettin' it. They moved him already. Didn't never know about it until he went toddling off there, but the Eyndar Empire's got two most wanted lists. A general-purpose one, and one for xenos. Blackjack Ramsey's the number 8 fella on the one, and tops on the other. It's on the feeds already. They're making a fucking holiday of it."

No immediate response was forthcoming.

"Captain? Captain...?"

"Shuttle 1 is aboard," Daphne reported from the command chair. "I think I'm going to get out of this chair now and hope it cools off before she notices we used it."

An angry intership comm from Logistics pinged red on Mindy's borrowed screen.

We just had Shuttle 1 park blocking the lift. Send someone tall enough to move it or we'll drag it out of the way with grav sleds.

If the captain was in such a rush that she made Grosstet park in a pedestrian and cargo lane, then—

"Get over here and take your post," Mindy warned, scrambling from Daphne's seat and racing over so as to be not quite occupying the captain's favorite chair.

Within seconds, the lift doors opened. "Ensign Galapap, maximum astral. Set a course for Trade Gate 4."

A "But, Captain" died unspoken on Mindy's lips.

―――――

The *Arete* hung at a comfortable 9.07 AU as Jessie's officers filtered into the briefing room. Just on the other side of the hull from them, Trade Gate 4 loomed. Despite her fury at the present circumstances in general, she had to admit that finding her ship's wizard loitering in the saloon, demanding instant transit to astral space, and the only reply being "pick a number" felt pretty good. She'd asked for nine, and the point zero seven was a rounding error that most astral authorities wouldn't balk at.

They came quick. They came in uniform. They came with whatever intel they'd scraped together in the four hours since the news had broken that Bradley Carlin "Blackjack" "Dad" Ramsey had been apprehended by Eyndar Imperial Police and transported to the homeworld.

It was time for a plan, and this was Captain Jessica Ramsey's planning team.

Commander Charlotte Webber. The *Arete's* executive officer was raised to be a pirate and trained as a wizard. She knew tactics and strategy as well as a graduate of Annapolis Prime. If she needed more motivation, her potential future father-in-law was the one in peril. And if Jessie needed suggestions about how to use magic in any plan, she could answer for the ship's little contingent of spellcasters.

Commodore Grosstet. Though subterfuge wasn't his specialty, Jessie had rarely met a sentient creature so brave and stalwart. And if he pulled some H-tech miracle out of his trunk and acted like they all should have known it existed already, it wouldn't be the first time.

Commander Trebla of Kethlet. Jessie's chief engineer could be the key to any jailbreak. If they needed to cut their way through eyndar tech to reach Dad, he'd be the one running the calculations.

Dr. Harmony Richelieu. Odds were good that the eyndar would mistreat their most wanted xeno in custody. Depending on how badly, they might have to include her in the rescue party.

Lt. Cmdr. Makket. Her Logistics chief and head of the

Support Division would be responsible for equipping the rescue effort with whatever they needed. From disintegrator rifles to modern eyndar police hovers, if Jessie decided they needed it, he'd be in charge of figuring out how to acquire it.

Acting Commander Lisa Schultz. With her brother's prolonged absence, Lisa was her head of Security for now. That put her in the crosshairs for intel efforts supporting the operation.

Kinniss Krow. Jessie's point of contact for the *Scylla*, the plouph security officer had been less than helpful in reconnecting Jessie with Aunt Jamie's ship. Apparently, they took operational secrecy to absurd lengths, and comm silence meant turning off even receipt of signals. Still, he was shrewd and experienced, and she couldn't justify excluding him.

Others, Jessie excluded with prejudice.

Ideas were great. Brainstorming sessions needed them. But she needed officers running the ship, and she needed few enough voices in the room that she could hear herself think.

"Here's what we know so far," she began once everyone was seated. "Carl Ramsey was taken about six hours ago. He was aboard a laaku-owned light freighter called *Shibi Shaaba*."

Trebla snickered at some wordplay in his own language, but a glare from Jessie shut him up.

"The ship was destroyed. Carl was picked up from an escape pod and taken into custody. The Eyndar Navy vessel *Rentak* delivered him to the homeworld, arriving within the past half hour."

"Been a bit wall-to-wall on the eyndar feeds.," Lisa reached toward the center of the table to tap several commands. The Briefing Room holo-projector sprang to life. A physical pain struck Jessie in the gut seeing Dad cooped up in a cage, slow-hovered down a major street with trash pelting the vehicle. Flares of a force field showed that they weren't going to let the crowd kill their prisoner before his assigned time. "Ain't current. From a bit ago, but they's loopin' it now. My eyndar's a bit squidgy, but sounds like a twisted-up bit of history they's puttin' out there for the prelims. Ain't much else to talk over meanwhile. On their part, that is."

A chastened Trebla piped up. "Don't worry, Jess. We'll get Uncle Carl back."

Jessie had heard the stories, once Dad was willing to admit to his past. Daring heists. Squadron 333 surviving suicide missions. Captured by pirates multiple times and escaped every one of them. But this time, the miracle fell on her shoulders, and the enemy was a civilization rivaling old ARGO. Sure, the Eyndar Empire lost every war, but it took a war for ARGO to stop them.

"Here's our starter plan. I don't expect this one to survive the echo of me telling it," Jessie began. "The basic idea: we show up over the homeworld, carve a 2-kilometer-deep trench around the capital city with the *Arete's* antimatter cannon, fly a shuttle down there, and kill anyone who tries to stop us leaving with Carl."

Kinniss raised a hand and offered a sheepish, fang-toothed grin. "A slight modification. Keep firing until the crust destabilizes. Retrieve your father amid the chaos of a planetary evacuation."

"I don't hate it," Lisa added, bobbing her head.

Grosstet gave a toot, demanding attention. "WE CANNOT DOOM MILLIONS TO SAVE ONE PERSON, NO MATTER HOW BELOVED."

"It would be billions," Kinniss assured everyone. "Their infrastructure is shit. Most of the population wouldn't get spaceborne in time."

Jessie gritted her teeth. She didn't need her crew feeding the bloodlust rising in her. The worst part was: this wasn't implausible. At least the part about causing a planetary cataclysm. Surviving when the eyndar turned their planetary defenses on the *Arete* and somehow managing to extract a high-value prisoner while the guards were in a panic both sounded far less likely to work out as planned.

"Give me options that don't involve genocide."

"Medical diplomacy," Harmony suggested. "Eyndar medical technology is decades behind Mars. Even their political elites still occasionally die of curable diseases. Their neurological research is more focused on interrogation than therapeutics. We'd just need to identify a favored member of the Eyndar Imperial Family with a treatable disease and offer a cure."

"Wouldn't *that* be lucky," Trebla snarked.

"It wouldn't have to be luck," Charlotte pointed out, sending a chill up Jessie's spine. "It would have to be someone well-liked enough that the emperor would feel the need to intervene. If he traded away a prize such as your father for some cousin or uncle, he'd be a ripe target for overthrow."

That was one of the problems with the Eyndar Empire. Jessie didn't even know the current guy. Emperor Hagraan had ruled before she and Eric leapt forward, but there had been two changes of rulership since then. Emperor Grudrak was just a name to her.

"Fair warning," Lisa announced, reaching for the holo controls again. "You're gonna hate this right off."

The newsfeed winked out, replaced by a holo still of an eyndar in flowing, over-decorated robes. "Princess Yaabu. Media drools over her. Public sees her as future empress material someday."

Jessie swallowed a lump in her throat. "She's... a puppy."

The eyndar in the holo couldn't have been more than six years old with perky ears and wide blue eyes. She'd let her tongue loll out for the holopic, which was considered highly rude among adults but sort of mischievous for a child. She wore her ceremonial robe with the hem rolled and tied just below knee level, like a peasant, leaving her legs free to run and play. Despite her prejudice against the eyndar in general, she could see why the public loved her.

"Yeah. But on account of whatever we do to her, they give your dad back and we undo it, it's all bridge water, innit?"

"I'm not infecting a child with anything," Harmony declared staunchly.

"Agreed," Jessie replied.

The meeting continued, with ideas bandied about wildly.

They could hold the planet hostage, similar to the starter plan, just with a finger on the trigger instead of squeezing it until the planet bled magma.

They could hold a press conference, where a fake Carl promised the galaxy that he was safe and all right.

They could offer to trade H-tech for Carl's safe return.

Meals came and went. Participants were excused to the washroom but not their quarters.

Multiple iterations of an assault plan slowly evolved into something Jessie considered might potentially work.

"All right. So, Niprakk Mol is eight hours from the homeworld. If we launch an assault there, and we wait until the four-hour mark of the response, and we can double back to the homeworld in half an hour..."

Trebla nodded. "Based on our 9 AU speed, it sounds like we'd have about three hours to get back and hit the prison with a strike team. Um, not-it for being *on* the strike team."

"I VOLUNTEER," Grosstet declared.

"I'll lead it personally," Jessie added. She scanned up and down the table for objections, but no one was keeping their captain off *this* mission. "I'd like to get two or three more volunteers, but I won't order anyone to come. There's a good chance we—"

The door slid open.

Hadrian poked his head in. "Captain. I need a word with you."

"Can't you see I'm busy?" Jessie snapped. "Whatever it is, it can wait. Wizard Charlotte is handling the—"

"Now."

The young wizard hadn't raised his voice. She couldn't tell if he worked magic, but with Harmony capable of stopping him and Charlotte at least able, in theory, to detect mind-controlling magic, she doubted that was at work.

Nevertheless, something about the way he said that one simple word resonated in her bones.

"Two-hour break. Set an alarm if you have to. I want everyone back here and ready for planning."

Jessie followed as Hadrian bypassed the lift and continued down the maze of corridors that all sloped and connected if you had the patience to walk far enough.

"Where are you going?" Jessie demanded, weary and sore. "I thought you wanted to talk to me."

"Yes. But only in private."

Hadrian marched forward, a snarl growing at the back of his throat. A few choice remarks to a captain, no matter how off-color or insubordinate, could be exchanged around a corner or in a lift car. For the conversation to come, a seat and a few beers were in order.

"This is stupid. Slow down. I'm not going to run to keep up with you. I demand to know what this is all about!"

Hadrian stopped in his tracks, sneakers squeaking. His

robes, already under a head of steam, billowed forward. "What this is all about? How about you getting your father killed?" Because he had developed a keen sense of the dramatic, he had come to that halt right in front of his own quarters. He slapped the door controls. "In."

"Where do you get off giving me orders? I don't owe you an explanation, and Charlotte's perfectly qualified to—"

"Jessica Judith Ramsey, march your ass inside and sit down."

She stiffened. Old memories clanked around that technologist skull of hers, but they recognized an authority that required no magic to exert. Jessie had developed the same reflex for obedience as the universe when it came to doing what he said.

Once both were inside, Hadrian shut the door.

"How did you do that? What magic did you—?"

"None. It's called willpower. Presence. Wizards have a bunch of words for it, but it's the confluence of wisdom and self-preservation that certain individuals develop if they're going to have a long life. I triggered a little bell in the back of your brain that told you I wasn't fucking around."

Jessie gulped. "Fine. But if you had anything to contribute, you could have done it in the Briefing Room."

"I reiterate. All your plans are going to result in Carl's death."

The girl playing captain in her little homemade uniform scowled at him. "How do you know what we had planned?"

"Your chief engineer is too much flappy-flap with the lips, as they say. He mentioned several leading plans, and I could envision the outcome of each. You have to remember that your father is a person. He's not a monument or a piece of technology to strap to a grav sled and fly off with. He's not a tactical objective; he's a sack of bones and blood that one quick squirt of a blaster can end."

"FUCK OFF," Jessie barked at him. "You barely know him. He's my—"

"I'm not finished," Hadrian continued. While he admired the fiery outburst as a sign of enthusiasm, he also disliked being thrown off his rhetorical stride. "I can get him out of there."

"You." Jessie echoed the word deadpan, with a mere flipping of a pronoun that would have made for the best canyon ever.

"I'll need a pilot, obviously. That's where you come in. We fly in. I'll grab Carl. We fly out."

"HAH! You and what magical army?" Jessie shook her head in disbelief at what she was hearing, and Hadrian couldn't really blame her. "No offense, but nobody is that good. I mean, maybe you're stronger than Eric now, but—"

"Look into my eyes."

Jessie resisted, but she couldn't help herself.

The world vanished.

Jessie found herself on a stone walkway—no, these were the battlements of a castle wall. She stumbled on the uneven footing, catching a booted foot and hearing a rustle of light chain as she steadied herself.

Her uniform was gone. In its place, she wore chain armor with a doublet over it. But the doublet bore the haathee face that had been woven into the *Arete's* uniform. Except, rather than come off a clothes printer, this one appeared hand embroidered.

Looking out over the wall, a medieval town spread before

her. Townsfolk drove carts of hay and sold fruit from stalls and paused to listen to streetside minstrels perform.

"What the fuck...?"

There must have been a malfunction in the haathee drones. Jessie was having a waking hallucination. She reached for her TeleJack to contact Harmony but found a steel bracer protecting her forearm instead. Her search for a datapad revealed a sword belted at her hip instead of pockets.

"You're not hallucinating," Hadrian told her.

Jessie spun to find the wizard behind her. And she'd have sworn she was alone on this wall a moment ago. He looked slightly different than before, though it was hard to put a finger on it. Older, perhaps. His robes had become ornate, regal, and imposing. Even the voice was subtly different. A little more gravelly but distinctly the same otherwise.

"What's going on here?"

Hadrian took her by the shoulders, and that's when she noticed he'd shrunk by a few centimeters as well.

"Believe it or not, I think your father's life means more to me than it does to you."

Jessie shook her head. "That doesn't make any sense. You've barely met him. I've known him all my life."

"Please allow me to introduce myself. I'm a man of neither wealth nor taste. I've been around for long, long years, and traveled the stars for most of them."

Jessie backed away, clutching the sides of her head. "That's Enzio's favorite Squadron 33 1/3 song... sort of. My head. This... where are we?"

Hadrian took a step to follow. "I read a book, and the buildings shook. Laid tracks with a troubador, and under my wing, the son he forsook."

Jessie snarled and thrashed her head back and forth. "No. Those *aren't* the lyrics. And you're not even singing."

"I watched with glee while your kings and queens, fought for sixty-four squares and you didn't care."

Jessie backed against the parapets and fought to wake up.

"I stuck around on a *Mobius*, when I saw it was a time for a change. Killed a lot of Carl's enemies until Amy swapped the game."

None of this made sense.

Was Jessie trapped in a waking nightmare, a magical prison, or had one of those little haathee drones done the neural equivalent of plugging a guitar amp into the ship's main engines?

"Pleased to meet you, Jessie. Hope you guessed my name."

She'd been listening. Not just to the butchered, spoken poetry corpse of a song. But to Eric. To her own gut instincts. To the wrongness in the universe. Somewhere inside, she'd realized when Hadrian had used her middle name.

"Enzio?"

Hadrian smiled benignly down at her. He offered a hand to help her up. "Close."

Even in this dream world, in her fairy-tale costume, Jessie found her mouth too dry to speak. On a second attempt, she managed to croak out, "Mordecai?"

She clasped the offered hand, and he pulled her to her feet. "Mordecai The Brown, at your service. But you can go ahead and call me Mort."

"So, Eric was right all along?"

"Little blabbermouth. My own fault, of course. But what was I supposed to do, let him be a failure at magic, too?"

Jessie knew that was a whole topic for another time, but for now she focused and reminded herself that a life was on the line. "Do you really think you're up to a solo rescue of Dad?"

Mort harrumphed. "I've been bailing your father's ass out of hot water for decades. But solo? No. Like I said, I need a pilot. I could rope the Ponytail Princess in on this one, but I lack convenient means to contact her. Besides, you're less annoying."

Ponytail Princess? "You mean Aunt Tiffany?"

"Forget her. And she's no more your aunt than I was your uncle."

"Yeah, but—"

"More of a grandfather," Mort mused. "Carl was like the son I never had."

"I thought you had kids."

The wizard's face twisted in a sneer. "Wasn't there to raise them right. Both turned out to be assholes. Met Cassie recently. Cold fish. Snobby. All the parts of her mother I looked past or didn't get turned against me. Cedric uncorked a genie and nearly wished the galaxy out of existence. And since he couldn't keep anything else corked, either, we both had to put up with Hadrian."

Jessie sprang back, suddenly realizing that this man, whoever or whatever else he claimed to be, was proudly claiming the identity of a mass murderer—albeit a close family friend. "What happened to Hadrian?"

"Oh, he's happy as a bunny rabbit playing emperor in Boston Prime."

Jessie didn't know how to respond.

"Stop overthinking things. Time's passing at a snail's pace. I can answer all your questions. But you can't tell anyone who doesn't already know."

"Who knows?"

"Your idiot father figured it out from ten seconds of conversation. Your brother added horse to square and idiot-mathed his way to the right conclusion. He may or may not have successfully kept the secret from Wizard Charlotte. And I was up-front with Sparta before she decided to get into a relationship with a wizard with thrice her years and a habit of swapping bodies."

"Is that it?"

"Well, Hadrian—that is, Emperor Khosrau—and his personal assistant Vincente know."

But Jessie's mind had already wandered off on its own. Who cared whether ten people knew or ten thousand? If silence was the price, Jessie would strike a deal with the devil himself. For the first time since hearing the eyndar had captured Dad, she felt like they had a real shot of getting him back.

She flung her arms around the wizard she'd once known as Uncle Enzio and burst out sobbing.

⌐══⌐

Trebla awoke to a blaring alarm from his datapad. In the darkness, he fumbled around over the edge of his hammock for the netted sack slung beneath. Fifty kilos of dead, snoring weight made it hard, but he wasn't going to wake Jasmine intentionally. It had taken months for her to even sleep through the night without waking from nightmares at least twice. Now, he felt privileged to discover she was a sound sleeper.

With some effort, a lower hand got a grip on the datapad. A quick tug, followed by a better grip, and he was able to give a flick and toss it to an upper hand within reach of his face.

He had a comm from Jessie.

Re: MEETING CANCELED

One-handed, he held and tapped and saw the message behind that promising subject line.

Preliminary plan settled. I'll be taking Hadrian on a covert op to free my father. Report to the Briefing Room at 0930 hours to work on details. Our 0130 *reconvene is canceled in the meantime.*

Nice. Succinct. On message. Allowed Trebla a decent night's sleep.

Until he noticed a big brown eye staring at the screen, too.

"Didn't mean to wake you."

"Looks like you've got all night."

"Yep." Trebla did his best to squirm into a comfier position. Jasmine made it easier by shifting her weight off him, sitting up and reaching for the overhead netting. A residual glow highlighted her curves as she retrieved a squirt bottle and took a quick drink.

"Good. You owe me from bedtime."

After tucking the bottle back into its woven slot, firm, strong hands pressed Trebla's shoulders down, sliding him to the middle of the hammock.

Brain still foggy from a couple hours of sleep with more on backorder, he seemed to recall demurring when Jasmine had propositioned him upon his return from the Briefing Room.

Trebla was exhausted, but he wasn't *that* exhausted.

Lisa's TeleJack zapped her awake. She must have slept through the auditory alarm. Her nightstand drawer contained a pop-top can that cracked open with one hand, a maneuver mostly seen against its beer-bearing brethren. EnerJuice Ultra was two night's sleep in a can, according to the adverts, and it was getting off easy with Lisa only asking for three quarters of one.

Mercenary life meant keeping odd hours. She'd gone fluffy aboard this pillow-soft starship. Gotten her hard edges smoothed out.

The taste of toothsoap and the chemical cherry flavoring

mixed like pickles and pudding. But it wasn't fair to the crew to show up breathing midnight tacos all over them.

As she brushed, Lisa checked a notification that had come in.

Re: MEETING CANCELED

One-handed, she held and tapped and saw the message behind that promising subject line.

Preliminary plan settled. I'll be taking Hadrian on a covert op to free my father. Report to the Briefing Room at 0930 hours to work on details. Our 0130 reconvene is canceled in the meantime.

"Oi. F'k mrph." She spat into the sink. "Fuck her, too. Yapping 'bout a two-hour nap, then sodding off and pushing the brief to reg'lar hours."

The EnerJuice Ultra coursed through her veins. She was exhausted, but Lisa's heart rate was up, pumping blood faster than she now either needed or wanted.

"And Hadrian... HADRIAN? The daft little blighter's gonna get his self killed and her along with him."

Then again, assuming a 0930 briefing didn't change the captain's mind, that took Lisa off the list of potential strike-team members. Not that she didn't want Carl back. But... well, there was a rescue mission, and there was a suicide mission going on about how it wanted to be a rescue mission when it was all grown up. Excepting that it weren't ever going to get a chance to grow up.

On account of the suicide.

Which Lisa, presumably, would not be participating in.

Fair trade for the lost night, all things considered.

———

Re: MEETING CANCELED

A custom AI personal assistant opened the text comm and scanned the contents.

Preliminary plan settled. I'll be taking Hadrian on a covert op to free my father. Report to the Briefing Room at 0930 hours to work on details. Our 0130 reconvene is canceled in the meantime.

Harmony continued sleeping until her standard 0600 alarm.

Grosstet stood waist deep in murky water, relishing the slight buoyancy that eased a constant pressure on his joints. Actually, he felt nothing at all from his collection of little aches that he didn't mention to others. He dipped his trunk and sprayed a shower over himself for the sun to bake away.

Glorious, glorious day.

His lakeside home lay just a short walk up the beach. Soon, he would return to mate with two or three of his visitors. In the afternoon, he'd be back to cool his loins once more.

A difficult life this was, indeed, being so in demand.

It took a herd to raise a child. And each one needed a mother. But the father could be anyone. The visitors awaiting him eagerly back at the house could have chosen a taller man or one with longer tusks than Grosstet to help them expand the herd. Instead, they chose to honor boldness.

A wise choice, and they would enjoy the length of their visit. Grosstet would see to that in the coming hours. And tomorrow as well. And the tomorrow after that.

He learned all their names, then forgot them a week after they left. It took effort, forgetting. An act of respect to the next aspiring mothers to join him here at the Lake With Small Waves and a View of Three Mountains.

As he soaked and relaxed, Grosstet moongazed. A paler white shadow against a pale blue sky, it would be gone before noon, and he would watch it depart.

A pair of unfamiliar ducks swooped in, perching one to each shoulder. New ducks were a blessing, and Grosstet found this development auspicious. Only a haathee living well could be so attractive that even ducks couldn't help but take note.

Then, the ducks quacked.

From afar, the sound of anatine vocalization was a pleasure. From so close that they could lift one's ears like window curtains, the noise became annoying quickly.

Grosstet warned them, "TOO LOUD, MY TINY FRIENDS. TREAD UPON ME OR SERANADE; DO NOT CHOOSE BOTH. FOR THE SAKE OF MY TRANQUILITY, RELENT!"

The ducks did not, however, relent. They synchronized.

"DRAT. NOT THIS AGAIN. I WAS ENJOYING THIS DREAM."

Grosstet awakened to find his alarm indeed pestering him to attend Jessie's next meeting. When he found that said meeting had been postponed, rather than return to bed, Grosstet ran a bath, resolving to do whatever he could to aid his brain in finding the Lake With Small Waves and a View of Three Mountains when he fell back asleep, soaking.

Charlotte was the first to arrive. The coffee she'd requisitioned had been delivered almost the instant she'd touched the comm panel to end her voice communication with the kitchen's cleaning staff.

A groggy Eric slumped in a corner. In all likelihood, his sister would shoo him away once the rest of the briefing attendees arrived. But he'd been so pathetic when she hadn't wanted to visit the Village of Eternity for an abbreviated respite that he'd stayed up alongside her instead of going alone.

Her own mental training allowed Charlotte to ignore the more onerous effects of fatigue. And it wasn't as if she'd been awake for days on end. She imagined that even without magic, she'd only have been a tad sleepy. Her beloved, on the other hand, slept like an ancient god, quick to slumber, troublesome to rouse, and often spoke strange tongues for a moment upon awakening.

The others were late.

A console in the table proclaimed the time as 0145.

"Wanna play twenty questions?" Eric murmured as a cup of coffee cooled before him, untouched.

"I don't think we're that desperate for entertainment."

"Nineteen questions?"

"Amusing..."

"Eighteen?" Eric pressed, giggling. Oh, this wasn't a good omen.

Luckily, Charlotte was rescued by the arrival of Makket.

"You're late, but you're the least offender of a sleep-sodden bunch."

"Commander-Webber-didn't-you-receive-the-captain's-comm-postponing-our-next-meeting-until-the-standard-0930-daily-briefing?I-was-passing-through-the-kitchen-when-I-was-casually-informed-that-refreshements-had-been-delivered-to-the-Briefing-Room-so-I-came-up-to-find-out-why-Apparently-the-captain-neglected-to-account-for-your-less-than-addictive-attitude-toward-communications-technology."

"Indeed," Charlotte replied coolly. Marching down the

length of the table, she took Eric by the wrist. "Come now. Back to bed with you."

Clad in a bathrobe and fuzzy slippers, the semi-comatose wizard meekly complied.

⸺

"Yes. Hadrian," Jessie clarified.

"You didn't even invite him to the meeting," Trebla pointed out.

Jessie wagged a half-eaten bagel at her chief engineer. "An oversight. It was late, and there will be plenty of time to bring him in on the planning phase. The Eyndar Empire might be a shithole, but it's a shithole with a huge military presence, and Carl's being held in their capital city. Plus..." With her non-bagel hand, Jessie activated the Briefing Room holo-projector.

All up and down the table, participants leaned in. Jessie's officers and one VIP guest studied the 3D rendering of a flat calendar.

"Extensive," Kinniss declared. He was the first, apparently, to fully absorb the contents. It made sense since he'd been operating in eyndar space the longest. He was naturally more familiar with their calendar system.

"That's one way to put it," Harmony commented. "I'd call it barbaric."

Jessie tried to divorce herself from the personal aspect at play here. The calendar on display described a week-long festival taking place leading up to the summer solstice. Carl being the main attraction of that festival had to remain a fact, not a feeling, or she was going to lose it.

"Six deaths *do* sound like about five too many, ya ask me," Lisa added. She shook her head and took a drink from her mug of coffee. "Them doggies got it bad for the old bugger, don't they?"

"According-to-the-Eyndar-Empire-official-omni-site-for-the-festival-the-Six-Deaths-is-a-time-honored-ritual-taking-place-over-the-course-of-six-days-The-deaths-were-once-near-death-torments-However-with-the-advent-of-modern-medicine-the-subject-is-expected-to-be-technically-dead-and-revived-five-times-restored-to-consciousness-and-at-least-a-semblance-of-mobility-before-the-following-day's-execution," Makket rattled off, reading straight from his datapad. "Since-we-fully-intend-to-render-this-celebration-moot-I-see-no-reason-to-delve-into-the-gruesome-details-of-each-death-individually-Suffice-it-to-say-that-the-omni-site-offers-graphic-depictions-of-each-and-I-must-say-artistic-license-aside-you-large-sentients-DO-seem-to-contain-a-great-deal-of-viscera-and-fluids."

"The last death," Kinniss explained, "includes a religious banishment of the soul from the afterlife. These guys don't fuck around when they hate someone."

Her father.

God, how Jessie wished she could have had a military career that would inspire such loathing in her enemies. And then, you know, not get caught by them.

Grosset squinted as he peered at Makket's datapad. "THERE APPEARS TO BE FOUR DAYS RESERVED FOR FAMILIES OF HIS VICTIMS TO TESTIFY."

"Yeah," Kinniss replied with a wheezing snicker. "Gets his ears talked off by a bunch of crying widows and orphans. Maybe we do him a favor and let him listen?"

"No worries, Jess. Your dad's a tough old bird."

Jessie shook her head emphatically. "He's not! He's friendly. He's clever. But he'll barely push a manual grav sled with his own amp and speakers on it if someone loads it for him. He lost teeth one time in a fight with a stuck refrigerator door. Sure, maybe he could fly back in the day, but now...?"

Trebla snickered. "Yeah. Heaviest thing he lifts nowadays are Aunt Amy's hips."

Jessie cocked her head as the Briefing Room fell silent. "Really? You thought now was the time for that?"

"I don't like this plan of you taking Hadrian and trying to sneak your way in and out of their top military prison," Harmony stated, wrenching everyone back to the topic at hand. "I think we're better off with a diplomatic approach."

A few taps at the console enlarged the holo-calendar. "You really think the people who turned their public relations people loose on a festival campaign are going to bargain away the main attraction?"

The doctor shrugged. "We'll have to make them a better offer. Violence doesn't solve every problem."

An echo tickled Jessie's mind. Something Uncle Enzio had said—more than once—though at the time, and coming from him, it had come out as a joke: *If violence isn't solving your problem, you're not using enough.*

Ha. Ha. Funny old Uncle Enzio pretending he's a big bad wizard again instead of a babysitter and part-time employee of a cultural nostalgia music act.

Those memories weren't as funny anymore.

"Well, if we pull this off just right, there will be hardly any violence. The Parade of Sorrow will start, and those fuckers will be missing the star of the show. We're going in blind right now, so our first task will be gathering all the intel we can assemble. Orbital traffic patterns and technology. Security protocols both in orbital and aerial space. Military presence. Police deployments. Schematics. Up-to-date street maps. Subterranean infrastructure. Dossiers on anyone we might encounter. We'll need to scout an insertion site and method. I want fleet deployments—pull them from Earth Navy Intelligence, not Mars. Those dictatorial fuckers can't count votes let alone enemy fleet strength. I want a total overhaul and scrub on Grosstet's shuttle. Outfit it for emergency medical care if we have to drag my father out in pieces."

She was huffing for breath and could feel the heat rising from the collar of her uniform by the time she was done.

"Any questions, come to me individually. No need to bog everyone down. This is priority number one. All the *Arete's* resources are at your disposal, plus what we can acquire."

As her senior officers filtered out, Harmony lingered. "You need to see me first."

<hr/>

Ten minutes later, Jessie was seated on an examination table in Med Bay in her undershirt. Harmony was busily attaching thin bands around her wrists, forearms, and biceps.

"This is new. What's the deal?" Jessie asked as she watched the process.

"They're high-precision neural scanners. Normally, they're used during rehabilitation or diagnosis of intermittent conditions. You can wear them days at a time with little interference with your daily routine."

"Days? What for?"

"I've been seeing transient cut-outs in your drone swarm. It's not something I'm taking lightly if you're going to be dropping down on the most hostile planet in known space and exiting with a prisoner in tow."

Jessie shook her head. "I'm in top shape. Never felt quicker or stronger. You want to try arm wrestling again? I'll flip you over the table before you budge me the other way."

"Uh huh... because the Eyndar Empire is going to arm

wrestle you." Harmony straightened and adjusted her datagoggles to clear and transparent with no visible data displayed, even backward. "I've seen your range scores."

Jessie scoffed. "Like all those perfect hundreds?"

"You've adjusted well to the new weight and balance of your body as it transforms. However, I've also seen the 70s. And I recall a 41 in there?"

"Flukes. Getting my bearings."

"Two days ago, Jess. Two."

The captain put up her hands in a rare act of surrender. She felt the bands' presence as her biceps flexed, though they didn't seem to interfere at all. "No mas. I'll wear the silly things if it'll make you feel any better. Now... if you don't have anything else to worry about, I'll just be—"

"I've arranged a workout to test your reflexes."

"C'mon, Harm. Now?" There were a million things Jessie needed to worry about. Any hiccups in her H-tech shit, Harmony would have plenty of time to iron out before the mission launched.

"Yes. Now. We're going to the gym."

"If you want to spot for me, fine, but—"

"The *other* gym."

Jessie cocked her head and accepted her jacket from the doctor as she slid off the table. "You can't think you're possibly a challenge for me. Unless those drones have replaced your muscles with servomotors, I've got to be twice as strong as you, and those drones are your only potential advantage. Skill-wise, I don't care what the plaque says, you won a game of rock, paper, scissors, not a martial arts tournament."

Before Jessie reached the door, Harmony had already gathered up a med kit and drone injector and slipped on a pair of sterile field bracelets.

"Overkill, much?"

"Daphne's waiting for us, and I told her not to go easy on you. I need to see how your body reacts in a life-or-death situation, and she's the closest we've got to a guaranteed thing other than roping in poor Grosstet."

Jessie snickered on the lift ride down. "Really? She's still an amateur. With my increased strength and enhanced reflexes, I don't see how she stands a chance."

Harmony didn't make eye contact, watching the doors as they opened at their destination. "Claws. Fangs."

"Hey, now. I thought we were talking about sparring here, not—"

"Plus, she's into her own strength regimen with two additional drone factories implanted. I don't have a solution for increasing the tensile strength of her claws without ruining the self-sharpening and growth features, but her fangs are harder than steel now."

Jessie didn't step off the lift.

"Come on."

"What the hell is going on here?"

Harmony regarded her through those datagoggles. Jessie wondered what that pale shimmer was showing her as she studied her captain. "We're going to get to the bottom of your drone malfunctions. It wasn't just the range where you seized up. I got the message when your self-healing routine repaired a Class 1 blaster scorch."

"It was nothing."

"It could have been. And it could be again if we don't get to the bottom of it. I need data I can't gather casually. Daphne is authorized to use lethal force to see if we can get the glitch to recur."

"WHAT?"

"The eyndar aren't the only ones who can bring a patient back from the far side. And I guarantee you, you won't wake up groggy from neural blockers if they do it to you. I don't care if you take Hadrian or Grosstet or even Eric, for goodness' sake, you're the risk factor in this mission until I know what's wrong with you."

Jessie gulped, wondering just how many bones Daphne might break of hers before Harmony got the data she needed.

What had possessed Eric to recreate this particular schoolhouse, he couldn't say. However, it met several criteria that he had in mind without having to think too hard. It was a small structure, just four classrooms and a few offices, plus an administrative desk up front. There wasn't much going on immediately outside, either in his memory or the more substantial recreation of that memory here in the Village of Eternity. And he'd spent a few weeks here when he'd stayed behind along with Ozzy and Mom while Jessie got to try a horseback riding program and Dad whizzed off to a gig on a nearby planet.

Real, actual memories had a fuzz to them. More recent ones, captured with a magical mind, were crisp by comparison.

Eric polished up this old memory until it gleamed. Extraneous detail was eliminated rather than clarified.

Simplify.

Simplify.

Simplify.

The clutter on the teacher's desk vanished. The mismatch of students' chairs became uniform red plastic with silvery metal legs. Rows of desks graffitied with markers and scratched with initials and doodles instead all shone with faux wood grain like the day the factory stamped them out. One pencil each. One sheet of paper each; Eric took the liberty of using real imaginary paper rather than imaginary plastisheet, despite the additional imaginary cost.

All four classrooms looked alike. Each had a green chalkboard with three pieces of chalk on a tray. Each had a placard across the top displaying the English alphabet. Above each door, a bell with an electrified clacker poised to ring like building-sized alarm clocks, regimenting the time within.

For months after attending this place—the real version, at any rate—Eric woke from nightmares of that sound.

To this sameness Eric added details to make each unique.

The children from those classes had long since faded beyond reconstruction. Charlotte had promised to help him someday reclaim all his memories back to birth. "A memory you'll never forget again," she called it. For now, Eric improvised.

A classroom with a mere twelve students was child's play to populate. A Dek here, an Ozzy there, a young tesud in datagoggles there was how he envisioned Uom'pe might have looked at 25 or so. He de-aged a Daphne to half her size and a Junior and Lisa, side by side in adjacent desks glaring blasters at one another. Jessie took a seat in the front row—which was a stylistic choice, not an accurate representation of where a Jessie would have seated herself.

Each student appeared to be roughly the equivalent of eight in human years. Around the time to learn multiplication and division. At eight actual years, most laaku would be on trigonometry, azrin would be settling down to start a family, and tesuds would be identifying shapes and animals.

Eric took his own seat, though his adult knees banged the underside of the desk. As all the other children sat politely attentive and waiting, he picked up his pencil and wrote in block letters on the paper before him:

IT ALL STARTS HERE

The bell rang, startling him even though he'd made it happen.

In stepped Dad.

Despite knowing Dad all his life, Eric had never seen his father wear a tweed jacket and bow tie combo. The horn-rimmed spectacles looked more like a holovid prop, especially since they clearly had no lenses in them. For today, he was playing the role of teacher, even bringing his own shiny red apple to place on the desk.

"Good morning, class."

"GoOoOd MoOoOrning Mr. RaAaAmsey," the class singsonged back in unison.

"Today, we will be studying Spaceship Crime," Dad announced, tapping out the words in chalk on the green wall slate with Dad's legendarily bad leave-a-note-on-the-fridge handwriting. "Who here can tell me about Spaceship Crime?"

The children all shook their heads and answered as a chorus. "We don't knoOooOw anything about SpaAaAceship Criiiime."

"Correct. But also, there's more to it than that. You see, part of crime—the most *important* part—is not getting caught. Who can come up with a way not to get caught doing Spaceship Crimes?"

Hands shot up. Dad called on students with a deftly pointed finger, eliciting answers one by one.

"Have an alibi," Little Junior answered, exchanging a nod with Little Lisa.

A Miniature Grosstet tooted in triumph when selected. "GET FAR AWAY FROM WHERE THE CRIME OCCURS."

"Eliminate witnesses," Young Jessie offered.

"Falsify, evidence," Baby Uom'pe suggested.

Dad had his back to the class, tap-squeaking with the chalk, documenting all the answers. "Great. Keep 'em coming."

"Don't commit crimes," Harmony said deadpan, drawing titters.

That got Dad to turn around, wagging a piece of chalk at the class clown. "How about we go with Abandon Bad Plans Before They Go Wrong," he read aloud as he wrote it on the board instead of her actual answer. All throughout the classroom, the other students dutifully mirrored the board's contents onto their papers.

"Keep some coppers on your payroll," a Tiny Mindy added. There were some "oohs" as she'd come up with a good one.

"All right," Dad stated as he set the chalk down. "But an important one I think we've all overlooked is contingencies. Can anyone tell me what a contingency is?"

Eric raised his hand and got called on. "That's when you have secondary, tertiary, or even more plans within plans to account for errors in the base plan."

"Whoa! Sounds like we've got ourselves a Mr. Fancypants Space Crimer right here. That's a great way to put it. What kind of contingency would you put in place for... the whole school catching fire?"

Eric knew before he smelled the smoke that this wasn't a hypothetical scenario. Out the schoolroom's one little window, flames had engulfed the colonial countryside. Children broke into a panic and rushed for the door, pounding fists when they found that they'd been locked inside.

A fire alarm rang that sounded exactly like the school bell.

And just like that, all the students were back at their desks, waiting politely with their blank paper and freshly sharpened pencils, ready to learn.

Eric double-checked his own paper.

IT ALL STARTS HERE

In walked Dad in his tweed and bow tie.

"Good morning, class."

"GoOoOd MoOoOrning Mr. RaAaAmsey," the class singsonged back in unison.

"Today, we will be studying Spaceship Crime," Dad announced, tapping out the words in chalk on the green wall slate with Dad's legendarily bad leave-a-note-on-the-fridge handwriting. "Who here can tell me about Spaceship Crime?"

Whether it had worked for real or only within the confines of Eric's mind, he had a nap's length out in the real world to determine. But to get there, he was going to first have to escape the trap he'd laid for himself and break free of what he could only hope was the failure-trigger time loop he'd been attempting to invent.

Sparta answered the door when Jessie knocked. She wore leggings and a crop top, the picture of collegiate leisurewear aside from the pirate's ransom in gold jewelry all that bare skin displayed.

"Oh, hello, Captain. To what do we owe the pleasure? Have you lost something? Or has something, perhaps, lost you?"

"Do you always have to sound cryptic?"

"No. It's just a perk of my order. Come on in. Hadrian is on a food errand. Should be back shortly."

Despite her ordeal, Jessie's stomach growled audibly at the news. She'd been gorging ever since Harmony had installed her drone factories. And the manufacturing was in overdrive as the system reacted to repair all the damage she'd sustained in the past hour.

"Mind if I take a seat while I wait?"

"Not at all. Can I get you anything? We have... beer... beer... and I think a little hard liquor. Oh, and some extra beer."

"Maybe I can order us up something. What's Hadrian bringing back? Maybe I can fill in some blanks."

"Oh, I wouldn't know. He said it would be a surprise. But he's making two stops. One for real food. One for that synthetic stuff the machine in the bar here makes. I've never had artificial food, and we're making a game of whether I can tell the difference."

The oracle seemed different. More relaxed. Maybe this was Jessie's first time actually meeting her for real. There really hadn't been time for casual socializing since she and Hadrian had gotten aboard—and Jessie was fully aware that she had the power to *make* such time and had chosen otherwise.

"I won't spoil it for you, then," Jessie declared. She flopped down onto the wizards' couch.

The door opened almost immediately thereafter, and Hadrian burst in, followed by a floating tram of dining-lounge plates. "The tesud woman wants these all back. Oh, hi, Jess. Come to share a bite? I know you can tell the difference between cooked and machined food, so you can't play the game."

"She knows I know?" Jessie asked.

"Merlin's beard, keeping secrets from this one is like fishing for anything *but* piranhas in a piranha-infested river. Easier to tell her just about everything." Hadrian set down his plunder on their kitchen table, and Sparta hurried over at once. "Uh uh. First, a reminder. No divination. Just taste and smell."

Sparta held up an oath-swearing hand. "I shall use no magic. Though if flashes of horrified cattle manage to bypass my protections, I bear no responsibility."

"Good enough. Take your pick."

Trapped by her own curiosity, Jessie forced herself off the couch on freshly knitted shins to watch up closer.

Four pairs of trays arrayed themselves with two versions each of hot dogs, ramen, tacos, and ice cream.

Sparta browsed, nose lifted to test the aromas as if she were a species with an actual sense of smell and not a mere human. "Just plain vanilla?" she asked with a feigned pout.

"Put too much junk in it, you'd tell in two shakes." Hadrian turned a glower on Jessie. "Speaking of two shakes, you look like you've been babysitting Kubu's brats. What happened to you?"

"Oh, this is nice..." Sparta declared, one spoonful into the bowl of vanilla. "Creamy. Sweet. Sol-grown beans if I had to guess."

Jessie cracked her neck, stretching out recently grafted ligaments. "Harmony wanted to prove a point that my nanobot drones weren't working. She doesn't think I should go on the rescue mission."

"Damned if I'm going to pilot myself there. And you didn't specify what happened to you; just why."

"Daphne beat the ever-loving shit out of me. Doctor's orders."

Hadrian harrumphed. "Never did see the appeal of scientific medicine..."

"She wanted to prove the machines are glitching out."

"I could have told you that."

"Ha. Ha. They're machines, so of course they glitch out."

The young wizard raised an eyebrow. "Did I really sound like that as Enzio?"

"No," Jessie admitted. "But that was your assigned impression. You knowing it was you was good enough for me."

"Well, then. Let me clarify, you—"

"Eugh! Ew! Ew, ew, EWWWW!" Sparta rushed to the

sink, spitting and leaving her tongue hanging out as she attempted to rinse off the residue. "That's the science ice cream. It was like putting the wrapper from a Freezi Bar in my mouth." She ventured to the freezer and drank straight from a bottle of whiskey.

"As I was saying... You're a wizard, so if you've got machines in you, it's no wonder you kerfuzzle them all."

Jessie grinned, despite the pain in her jaws from six new teeth. "Been a while since I heard that one. But you should know better. I'm no wizard. That trick with the reflexes isn't actually *magic*, it just seems like it."

"No. It's magic."

"Eric's the wizard in the family."

"Eric wanted to be one. He worked at it. You're a natural. Those reflexes of yours are like your mother's."

"Yeah. I know. Great on the firing range and in the cockpit. Just like Mom. But that's a far cry from wizardry."

Hadrian took a bite of a taco and handed the other to Jessie. Sparta had already picked out the Uom'pe-made ramen and turned that into her meal. For her part, Jessie could tell she'd been given the machine-made, protein-sculpted taco made from laaku goo. She, however, didn't care. Raised on junk food and pub fare, she'd eaten so much worse without complaint.

"Jessica, your mother didn't want you to know because she found knowing such a burden, but while Eric has managed time travel, you see the future regularly."

"What? No. I just react unnaturally fast—maybe. It's no more magic than sleight of hand. Except my eye is quicker than most hands, and my hands are quicker than my own eyes."

Hadrian folded his arms, leaving half a taco hanging unattended. "Lemme guess. Your difficulties arise when you need a quick reaction."

"That's a lot of the time."

"My point exactly," Hadrian declared triumphantly. "You know what? I've been wanting to teach you some shit for years. Your mother forbade it. I had Eric as an apprentice, so I let it drop. Figured you'd get a chance to decide when you turned eighteen. Then you up and shipped yourself into a uniform, and I haven't seen you since."

"Sorry..."

"Couldn't tell whether I was prouder or more pissed off that with the resources of Earth and its colonies at my disposal, I couldn't even get you back to Earth without admitting who I am."

Jessie ground her teeth. *She* remembered that chase a little differently.

"Anyhoo. You keep your blood full of bulldozers or whatever—"

"Little frogs, I thought," Sparta chimed in unhelpfully.

Hadrian continued without pause, "—and you'll keep ruining whatever it is they're doing."

Jessie felt her head swimming. "But I've just really started getting used to them. I'm so much stronger, faster, tougher."

"And yet, a lumbering furball who was playing piano down in the saloon ten minutes ago when I was there, just 'beat the ever-loving shit out of you'?"

"That's different."

"The eyndar will be different. They won't hold back or stop when Dr. Know-Little calls them off. If you want to be my pilot to rescue your father, you've got a choice. Get those dooz-a-jiggies yanked out of you and just be Jessica Ramsey, Earth Navy assassin—"

"Special Forces."

Hadrian had a way of glancing away in disdain and waving away her argument that conveyed "po-tay-toe, po-tah-toe" clearer than words ever could. "Or I can teach you some tricks that'll make Harmony's tech seem like kiddie toys."

Jessie chewed her taco as she considered. "What kind of tricks?"

The grin that preceded his answer reminded her that Hadrian had known Jessie all her life. He knew he had her already. "Stop by here before you turn in for the night. I'll show you."

<hr />

Darts flew. A kitchen cutting board slap-taped to the wall and spray tinted with concentric rings took the impact. Serifos Supply Depot had been overrun, and the inmates were running the prison. Captain Jamie Ramsey breezed past the mess hall, carefully avoiding eye contact with any of her crew as they made their own fun in the cramped quarters of the depot.

Kenny, in tow, was less inclined to overlook the affronts to cookware, power systems, and cleaning supplies.

"Your crew's tearing up the place."

"What can I tell you, Kenny?" Jamie shot back. "We limped here after a firefight, and you had a slot for us before the dust settled. Some of us wouldn't mind a peek at how our dust is faring." She cut him off as he was about to speak. "I know. I know. I'm not looking for an exception. I'm just explaining why they're all on edge."

"Yeah? Well, this is all going on your bill."

Being reminded of exorbitant sums she was already on the hook for, Jamie hardly cared. "Look, you want this place cleared out, get the rec room on the *Scylla* vacuum rated again. I'll gladly send them over there. I'm sure they'd rather have an actual Ping-Pong table and holo-chess than making shit from your cupboards."

Frankly, she admired her engineering staff's ingenuity in putting together working toys and sporting equipment to keep the crew as amused as they were. She'd ushered them all off the *Scylla* in a hurry so that the Serifos people could get started immediately. Most had left their quarters with a change of clothes and a toothbrush and little else.

Grumbling about tripping over unauthorized personnel, Kenny ambled off to take care of his own business rather than continue nagging Jamie about hers. Quiet space was damn near impossible to find, short of a washroom stall, but a captain could manage a few tricks.

Still, a captain also attracted problems like lakes attracted tourists. You could post all the "Do Not Disturb the Serenity" signs you wanted, but everyone liked to think a sign like that was to keep everyone else away.

The latest to misread Jamie's signs was Jaxon.

The *Arete's* security chief cornered her in an alcove meant to provide access to the station's plumbing junctions. She was puffing a light cannabis mixture from an atomizer when he made his move.

"Captain, got a minute?"

"What is it?" she did her best not to snap. The smoke had barely hit her lungs and definitely hadn't soothed raw nerves quite yet. And she had about eleven minutes, last she checked, before Sofia was supposed to meet her here for a check of her own plumbing junctions.

"I've had a lot of time to think. Once we get back from comm silence, I was wondering if maybe I could request a transfer?"

"We're not a military. We're two independent ships who cooperated on a mission. Plus, I've already got a security chief."

Jaxon shook his head. "I don't care about rank. I did the job because no one over there was qualified. Including me, if I'm honest. Look. I get it. You barely know me. But you're a legend. And you've been out here forever, doing shit about problems no one else seems to care about."

"Jessie cares," Jamie assured him.

"Jessie's in over her head and content to stay there. And ever since the you-being-a-future-version-of-her incident, she's hardly looked at me."

"Did I ever apologize for that?" Jamie asked, genuinely unable to recall. Knowing herself, she could have seen it either way. But whether she said it or not, she really wasn't sorry. She just knew that the two of them were doomed. Successful relationships came in a million flavors. But doomed ones followed a few standard archetypes.

Jamie hadn't gotten to where she was in life without picking up a lot of insight into the sentient mind. What Jaxon had with her niece was comfort sex. Two paranoid shitheads sating their lust with someone they were comfortable falling asleep next to without worrying about murder. Every couple needed *something* in common, but neediness, insecurity, and post-traumatic levels of paranoid was building a foundation out of explosive precursors.

"Nothing to apologize for. Scraped a layer of tint off so we both saw the rust underneath. But it also makes going back awkward. If you don't need me, fine. I'll go back to finding work on my own. Don't know if Lisa will come with or not. Probably. She's like that. But I won't find anything doing *important* work. Not like the *Arete* or the *Scylla* are doing."

"Got a taste of the good life?" Jamie asked with a smirk.

Jaxon barked a laugh. "This is the good life?" He looked around meaningfully. "Covert repair bases and life-or-death firefights? Jumping from one rescue mission to the next with—correct me if I'm wrong on this one—no pay?"

Jamie was quiet a moment. She took a puff. "We scrape

something together for retirees. Make sure they're OK out there in the galaxy. Most of us retire the hard way in this life."

"And you still call it the good life?"

Jamie smiled sadly. "The only good life. Find your people. Fight by their side until you've got no fight left. Pass on the fire to someone who still does."

"I thought maybe I found my people, but it turns out I'm still looking."

"Fine. Kinniss will put you to work when he gets back."

"Chik-ta has been wanting to say something, too."

"I already accepted him," Jamie replied. "Sessilla had been trying to incubate her clutch in a goddamn toaster oven. She's got a cousin back home willing to raise the brood when they hatch, but she didn't want to leave the eggs. Chik-ta's pretty sure she's going to have five hatchlings in a couple months and be looking to move on. Cousin's going to have to find her own, he's betting."

Jaxon bobbed his head. "You won't regret this."

A quick check of her chrono rekindled Jamie's ire. "I'm regretting it already. I've got a date, and you lingering around here with that Medium Penis Energy of yours is going to ruin it. Shoo!"

Harmony adjusted her datagoggles, overlaying a three-dimensional view of Medic Britney Daschel's skeletal system corresponding to the constant scans from the examination table. Her patient squirmed slightly in an apparent attempt to get comfortable prone with her face supported by a cushion that allowed her to see the floor and both breathe and speak freely.

"You could have kept your clothes on," Harmony

mentioned offhandedly. She'd been taught that light conversation both put a patient at ease and helped establish a mental state. However, a slight case of nerves was always to be expected prior to surgery, and Medic Daschel's mental state could be inferred from her heart rate and neurotransmitter levels.

"All good here, Dr. Richelieu. I've been on the other side. Easiest patient's nude as an anatomy lab holo. Smocks and gowns and all that's just for modesty. I've got none to worry about. Let's just do this."

"And, for formality's sake, do you, Britney Marissa Daschel, consent to the experimental procedure outlined in the medical information packet provided, in summary, the installation of four additional Harmony Tech drone fabrication devices?"

"Yep."

In her goggles' view, Harmony could already see the factories she'd be installing, ghostly as opposed to the pair Britney had already been growing acclimated to. The two in her spine would be joined by a pair in the femurs and two at the base of her skull.

"Do you consent to the aftercare regimen outlined in that same document? Namely, the significant dietary alterations, physical and mental testing plan, and remote monitoring?"

"Yeah. All that. Same as the first time but more."

Same as the first time, except Harmony had added a number of waivers to counter Jessie's whining. The drones would be proactively counteracting any attempts to alter brain chemistry through recreational chemicals. They would hunt down and quarantine harmful food additives before the digestive tract absorbed them. Ninety percent of the contents of a Snakki Bar would be excreted as tiny pellets that the liver and kidneys would never need to be bothered with. Sleep cycles would be carefully regulated, with vitals monitoring and external alarms given permission to decide when waking up mid-slumber was worthwhile.

Her assistant would eat healthy if she wanted to avoid hunger, would sleep soundly and awaken full of energy, and wouldn't fall prey to the easy allure of chemical addictions. If she needed therapy, she could get it by talking to a therapist rather than checking bottles to see if peace of mind was at the bottom of one.

In short, Britney was perfect.

And about to become more perfect.

"And, lastly, you acknowledge that if you attempt to profit from this technology, allow anyone to reverse engineer it, or act against the interests of Harmony Corp or the starship *Arete* and its crew, that the devices will remotely disassemble themselves."

"Honestly? I'd like to see how that all works. But, personally, yes. I'm not going anywhere. I'll have to break the news to Captain Ramsey—Jamie Ramsey, that is. But I'm here as long as you'll have me."

Harmony had made the first incision as soon as that statement included a definitive affirmative. The procedure was becoming old hat, too. Aside from having quite a lot of muscle to cut through when accessing Medic Daschel's femurs, it was the same thing as always.

"Do you mind me asking?" Harmony mentioned midway through the second femoral factory installation. "What prompted you to want a second round of upgrades?"

"The strength is great," Britney replied. "Don't get me wrong. Reminds me of how I felt in the corps, minus that pervasive haze that felt like my brain had a layer of food-safety wrap keeping me from getting morals all over my nice clean brain. But I've been a big girl all my life. I stand out in a crowd."

"This isn't going to counteract that," Harmony pointed out.

"You may slim down some with more efficient muscle tissue, but you'll still be fit and brawny. And you'll still be over 1.9 m tall."

"I get that. Been nice having Sparta around. Girl I can look in the eye. Did you know she's never played basketball?"

"I didn't."

"I wanted to join my school's forensics team. You know. Public speaking and debate. Maybe get used to being the center of attention. But my mom thought I'd get a scholarship if I went out for rugby. So, after a long talk, I spent two years in JV, two mostly on the bench in varsity, and got zilch for scholarships."

"Ouch."

"Heh. You're not the one with her legs cut open."

"We're on to your occipital implants," Harmony countered. With the neural blocks in place, and a light hand, she was pleased that her patient hadn't even noticed.

"Wow. Bonzer! That was quick."

Harmony also noted that, while she rarely used that old slang anymore, her occasional slip to youthful patois hadn't gone unnoticed.

"The more we perform the procedure, the easier it will get. I imagine that after your neural upgrades are stable, we can start training you on the installations."

"Really? Me?"

"Why not? You're not a static set of skills. You'll learn. You'll improve. That's what all this is about."

There was a sniffle. "You don't know what this means to me. I was always smart. Not, you know, smart like you. Just... regular smart. But all anyone saw was a gal who could throw some of the guys around but still got to play on the girls' teams. My rugby coach was decent. She felt bad I didn't get accepted anywhere. But the brainy schools didn't put much stock in mediocre athletes with no other hobbies they could nail to an application. The sporty schools obviously didn't give a care. Coach Brooke pointed me to a marine recruiter."

"Failure of the Phobos education system."

"Mind me asking? What'd you do in school? I mean, like, after school when you were a teenager."

"Everything," Harmony replied. "My family had money and both my mothers knew the pitfalls of an unsupervised childhood. My time was scheduled until spare numbers burst out of the seams of the chrono. I did track and field, football, swim team. I took three different self-defense classes. I was a Junior Science Meet semifinalist and almost ended up representing Mars. Summers, I worked. I was twelve, I'd earn fifty terras spending money babysitting and get picked up in a ten-million-terra hover by my chauffeur. I was lifeguard at a beach resort where my school friends would stay. By sophomore year, I was already sampling college courses. By junior year, my summer internship was in Harmony Bay community outreach. I didn't learn what boredom felt like until college."

"Wow."

"It's less 'wow' when you're in the middle of it. It gets exhausting. But I never learned how to relax. I see people do it, but I just struggle."

"I don't want to relax," Britney replied. "I want to do more."

"You can start by sitting up," Harmony advised. She handed her assistant a pile of neatly folded clothing that she'd been wearing upon arriving at Med Bay for her surgery.

Britney nodded a quick thanks and tugged on her uniform in a flurry of military precision. "Never get over the nerve blocks you guys have here. I've been patched up a bunch. Always felt a little something, even if it was dull."

"I make a point of not restoring nerve function until the

tissue is healed. The difference you're feeling, however, is approximately 20 seconds of drone work eliminating residual inflammation."

Britney twisted, regarding the backs of her own thighs as best she could manage before pulling up her pants. "Amazing. Can't even see the scars."

"I could get rid of the rest, you know. Or you could, with a little more training in drone programming."

Britney rubbed the back of her neck. Whether she was attempting to find the incision sites or not, she appeared abashed. "Thing is... I earned those. Each has a story. Like... if I healed over them, I'd forget. GNN offered me a correspondent job, based on that vid we made on Ghenlar Par'Mol. Said I'd need to clean that all up, plus, you know... the smile." She grinned for effect, showing off a slight gap. "Guess you had magnetos as a kid. Mom didn't think it would work too good playing rugby..."

"Nope," Harmony replied with a weary sigh. "Perfect as they've ever been. Perfect as Xrista's will be."

"You looked ahead? Some kind of pre-gression algorithm?" Britney sounded both impressed and eager to learn.

If she was going to be around for the long term, maybe the very long term, Harmony would need to trust her with worse secrets than this.

"Not exactly. Follow me."

From the examination room, they headed to Harmony's office, where she opened the hidden incubation chamber.

"Wow, that's been in your wall the whole time?"

"No. I had it installed."

When the cool steam dissipated, she wiped the alloy glass free of condensation.

"That... that's..."

"Eight month's gestation. Paused, presently. I'll finish her up when I've told Jessie and decided on a name."

"How... I mean... Who? I mean..."

"She's a clone of me. Same as Xrista. It's an evolution of a technology someone forced one of Harmony Bay's research teams to develop over twenty years ago. I've refined it. I've never been pregnant. Never plan to be. My family will be exactly the size of my choosing, with the DNA of my choosing. I've... never even had a serious boyfriend."

"Too busy, eh?"

"Something like that," Harmony muttered, unable to take her eyes off the beautiful little sister Xrista would soon have.

A hand on Harmony's shoulder pulled her into a side hug. "They're overrated. You made the right call.'"

———

This was like the worst of her teenage dating life. Showing up at some guy's house, waiting for his parents to open the door, judge the shit out of her, and silently decide if she was good enough for their kid or too easy. When the roles were reversed, sappy teenage boys had brought flowers. Jessie rarely ended up with a second date with any guy who offered flowers on the first. But when Jessie did the knocking, she had an old standby that somehow felt appropriate once again.

The door to Hadrian's quarters slid open.

Sparta stood just on the other side and must have noticed when Jessie's eyes widened. "Yes. I live here. And guessing who is on the far side of doors is something of a professional hazard. Come on in."

"I... uh... brought beer," Jessie replied, following through on her scripted greeting despite finding the lady of the house was on site. She lifted a plastic-bound six-pack of Brummstimme Lager.

"Great," Hadrian called out through the open washroom door. "Just like old times."

Jessie remembered. It wasn't that long ago, really. By writ and decree, all beer aboard the *Mobius* belonged to Uncle Roddy. But that didn't stop everyone else from drinking it, except for Aunt Shoni and the cousins—besides that one emergency trip to the detox center after Dek tried one. Offering someone a beer was a service, not an exchange of goods, but it was also an act of goodwill.

And it was the primary way Eric bribed Uncle Enzio into teaching him more magic tricks.

"Two apiece," Sparta declared, reaching and snapping one free of its bindings, leaving Jessie holding a five-pack. "How egalitarian."

"I didn't know the protocol," Jessie replied lamely. "Eric always used to bring you a beer."

"Unnecessary to the process. Just a kind gesture. Makes me wish I'd skipped the toothsoap, but these damned baby teeth are so damnably white it seems like a shame to let them rot."

"Two beers ought to more than rinse away the aftertaste," Sparta asserted, handing over the first beer as Hadrian emerged in pajamas and bare feet, then prying free another for herself.

"So, how does this work? I remember something about booze loosening up the mind for magic."

Hadrian scoffed. "If you need your name sewn into your britches, sure. But for anyone worth teaching, it just gets in the way. It's like learning to box with a sledgehammer. Sure, it works, but it's not preparing you to actually *box*."

"What, then?" Jessie inquired.

Hadrian cracked open his can and took a drink, nodding in

approval. "Easiest way is a quick nap. You know that place I showed you, where I admitted my true identity?"

"Not liable to forget it anytime soon," Jessie promised.

"Eye contact is the quickest way there. But it dries the old eyeballs out something fierce if you stay too long. Physical touch you can maintain for hours, but it's harder to take someone unwillingly."

Sparta circled around to the far side of the bed. "Normally, I prefer to travel there fully nude and pressed the length of Hadrian's body. Tonight, we'll hold hands and wear pajamas."

"You'll... be joining us?"

Hadrian chuckled. "Look. I've had my share of aspersions cast my way. Esper spent months sleeping in my bed on the *Mobius*. I was twice her age, and she came across as naive back then."

"Still does," Jessie grumbled.

"With Tiffany, I had to be more circumspect. Everyone thought Enzio was a creep thanks to being a Rucker deserter and Tanny's kept man. But nothing ever happened with either of them. By the time I was teaching Eric, I could accelerate time faster. A little staring contest here or there was long enough to train him."

"So how long will this take?"

Sparta sat on the side of the bed and crooked a finger to beckon Jessie over. "Just lie down. You're captain, and we're all adults. It'll take as long as it takes."

Hadrian slid himself under the blankets and over to the middle of the bed, where a gap between two pillows didn't seem to—

Sparta fixed the situation immediately, shoving her pillow under Hadrian's head and curling up on his chest. The tall, slender wizard flapped a hand, summoning Jessie over.

"Come on. Shoes off. Wear anything else you like. She's the

snuggly one. Just lace your fingers with mine so we don't slip apart accidentally."

When she lifted a beer and Hadrian voiced no objection, Jessie proceeded to chug the contents. Then, wondering just what she'd gotten herself into, she climbed into bed beside the wizards and intertwined her fingers with Hadrian's.

She'd barely had time to throw the blanket over herself—in a uniform and stocking feet—before the bed, the room, and the entire starship *Arete* plummeted away beneath her. Only her grip on the young-looking wizard tethered her as she fell.

━━

Jessie appeared upright and standing in her socks, still fully uniformed. The room around her was open-air, supported by wooden pillars painted a glossy red. From beneath the timber and tile roof those pillars supported, she had a view of a castle and surrounding town spread far below. They were up on some mountain, by the look of things.

Taking in her more immediate surroundings, Jessie sleepwalked across a woven fiber floor with ancient-looking weapons stored on finely crafted racks of polished dark wood. At the center of the room, tinted onto the floor, was a circular design of four stylized fists punching in a clockwise direction toward one another.

"What is this place?" Jessie asked.

Mort appeared as if her question had summoned him. He wore the ornate black robes she'd seen him in on her previous visit to his mind. "Welcome to the Temple of Four Fists."

Jessie grinned in recognition. "Wait a minute. This is from that shitty old holo of Uncle Roddy's, isn't it?"

"This is a wizardly recreation of a Hollyworld adaptation of a laaku script of a Japanese dojo as it might have appeared if the ancient laaku had visited Earth around the sixteenth century and been unable to tell samurai and Shaolin monks apart, then added monsters to make it more fun."

"Seriously?"

"No. Not really serious at all," Sparta chimed in. Jessie hadn't noticed her appear. While Hadrian had gone for Mordecai The Brown's body and a fashion glow-up, Sparta had turned herself into a goddess. Her skin had drained of color and shone like polished porcelain. Her irises had gone so pale that they barely distinguished themselves from the whites around them. An elaborate coiffure lent her the impression of wearing a royal crown. The gown the wizard wore could have been wound from the single strap of fabric the width of a hand, both completely modest and tantalizingly suggestive at once. "We come here to play."

"Play..." Jessie echoed.

"Oh, we all have our own ideas of fun," Sparta assured her.

Mort stepped in. It was hard to decide whether to consider him Mort or Hadrian or even Enzio. He was both all of them and none. Like the temple, he was an impure mixture with no solid identity. "You mentioned Roddy's taste in holos. How much did you ever watch them?"

"The fight scenes, mostly," Jessie admitted. "Pretty blasty, even if you learn in baby's first karate class that it's all bullshit."

"You remember the main character?"

Jessie wracked her brain and winced. "Sorry."

"That is quite all right," a new voice said with stilted formality. "I take no offense."

Jessie found the fucker from the holos standing right behind her, perched on a wooden staff that angled to the floor as he held on at arm's length, a feat of impeccable balance—if this place had been real.

"Jessica Ramsey, meet Bentho of The Temple of Demon Punching."

Wrapping a palm around a fist, she sketched a bow. "It's an honor to meet you." She turned to Mort. "I don't know what this is about, but I already know a *lot* of martial arts forms. I'm a certified Earth Navy close combat instructor."

"Lay one fist upon me, and I will accept that you have nothing to learn from me," the fictional laaku taunted.

"Yeah. Right. You and that staff aren't going to let me close enough."

Bentho flexed the staff, and when it straightened, he sprang atop it, balancing on one hand with the staff perfectly vertical. "One punch. One kick. One blow from this very staff. Try me."

As he dropped to the floor, the master flung the staff toward Jessie, spinning end under end.

She caught it without even thinking, without taking her eyes off him for a second.

"Fine. Have it your way." She slipped out of her socks and took off the jacket of her uniform.

Earth Navy wasn't big on staff forms, but Jessie had studied here and there on her own long before enlisting. She whirled through the Yin Shou Gun form as Bentho circled out of reach.

"Basic..."

Jessie switched up and showed off some wushu techniques she'd picked up.

"Sloppy..."

She wasn't going to stand here letting this fictional punk talk shit all day. "Yeah. Well, let's see you hit me."

"If the student wishes, I will demonstrate."

Bentho hopped, sprang, and cartwheeled with an ease no human could match. But he was still laaku. One of the key tenets of interspecies martial arts was understanding the matchups. The low laaku center of gravity was great for agility but the height and reach advantage went to humans. Jessie knew her reach with a bo staff and attempted to keep the laaku master at just that range.

Easier said than done.

The laaku had no respect for the threat she posed. As fast as she could change the direction of her strikes, he shifted faster. As quick as her reflexes allowed her to react to his moves, his anticipation defied belief. The very wind of her attacks seemed to blow him clear.

Then, when he sprang too high avoiding a low sweep, Jessie knew she had him.

Up came her staff, ready to catch him as gravity pulled Bentho down in a predictable arc.

But rather than fall, the laaku master hung suspended in midair for a fraction of a second, then lanced toward her, a lower hand leading with an open palm that struck like a haathee's trunk.

The bo staff clattered to the floor. Jessie pinwheeled through the air. When she hit one of the wooden pillars, it cracked from the impact.

To her astonishment, Jessie only had the wind knocked out of her.

"How...?"

"I've rendered you indestructible," Mort explained. "This crazy fucker would kill you as soon as train you. So I took precautions."

"Master Mordecai is all-powerful," Bentho acknowledged as he wandered over, toting Jessie's staff. "But you are pathetic. Unworthy. Come find me again when you're stronger."

"What the...?" Jessie shook her head to clear it. "Is that it? That's all you've got for me?"

Bentho stopped in his dramatic sauntering departure and

turned ever so slowly to regard his would-be pupil. One eyebrow arched.

"Yeah. You heard me." Jessie climbed to her feet. "Get back here so I can clobber you." She raised her hands in a guard position.

"Ah. Muay Thai. Inferior." Bentho clasped his upper hands with one of his lower ones behind his back.

Jessie wasn't going to let mind games get the better of her. She raced forward, ready to low-kick this asshole's ribs out his backside.

A twist, a duck, her leg caught nothing but air. Time and again, and the laaku didn't even appear winded.

Then, instead of one of his dodges, Jessie found one of her punches met with a faster one. A lower hand caught her in the solar plexus even as the rest of Bentho slipped past her fist unscathed. That open-palmed attack struck like a cannonball.

Jessie rocketed through the air, woven floor just out of reach to arrest her momentum. She crashed through a wooden railing and into open air beyond.

She screamed as the mountainside yawned below her, dropping away as Jessie's flight continued outward bound.

This is a dream. This is a dream. This is a dream... she chanted to herself in an effort to awaken before the ground rushed up and splattered her.

Freefall was like zero-G training, except there, no one was accelerating to lethal speeds.

Down, down, down Jessie plummeted, breath coming quick once she'd stopped herself from screaming. At any second, she expected to wake drenched in sweat beside two wizards looking to get themselves booted off her starship.

Jessie hit a tree in the forest at the mountain's base, punching through leaves and snapping branches. She struck the trunk of another, shattering it with bone-crunching force.

But her own momentum slowed. Tumbling in an uncontrolled fall, she broke smaller branches and ricocheted off larger ones. The soft forest soil might as well have been sacks of permacrete for all the comfort its impact brought.

She hurt all over. However, miraculously, a quick self-check revealed nothing broken and little blood.

"*AGAIN!*" a laaku voice thundered across the countryside.

"Seriously?" Jessie asked in a normal tone, unsure whether her lungs even had a shout in them.

"Yeah," Mort replied, stepping from behind a nearby tree. "You impressed him with your persistence, but you'll lose him if you don't skedaddle back up that mountain. There are stairs. Fifteen thousand some-odd."

"That'll take hours. I don't have that kind of time to waste."

Mort leaned in. "You've got decades until morning. *Vade.*"

"Wah-day yourself. I'm not wasting all that time trudging up that mountain. Whoosh me up with magic."

Mort snickered. "I could, but the training is part of the learning process. Your muscles out there won't get anything out of the exercise, granted, but you'll toughen up mentally."

"I'm plenty tough mentally."

The wizard arched an eyebrow. "You've got one little magic trick at your disposal, and you do it by instinct. You're the equivalent of a facial tic the universe doesn't even know it's got. If you figure out what *actual* toughness means, you'll be able to not only kick that monkey around like you've got him in a pinball machine, but you'll be able to do the same back in the land of beer and blasters."

"For real? You mean fight like Aunt Tiffany does?"

"I taught Esper basic stuff. Body control. Telekinesis. She figured out a bunch of stuff for herself. But she's honestly not much of a fighter. Decent enough wizard, but her fighting is mostly magic. Tiffany... she was a spoiled brat before I taught her anything. Bit of bloodlust in her, if I've got to be honest. She could kill with fire and lightning if she felt like it, but she seems to enjoy breaking people with her bare hands. That makes her a killer; take away magic, and you'd beat her to a pulp. I don't see you ever matching either of them as a *wizard*-wizard. But you'll be able to hold your own against anyone in hand-to-hand combat—and I mean even Daphne and Grosstet —once you master the art of Spirit Fist Magic."

Jessie's brain latched on to something familiar. This fell within her rudimentary grasp of Kejathi.

"Kip-tie-mahl?"

Inballi was one of the smallest worlds Eric had ever created. One could see the other side of it from any outdoor space. Mystical lamps provided light at all hours, and they turned off in sequence to provide a semblance of day and night. Otherwise, Eric would have had to plunk a sun down in the center, and that would have ruined so much of the charm. For Inballi was, of course, a world inside a ball.

Trying out this novel world was a privilege reserved for a scant few souls who'd been living particularly kind lives of late. The result was a delightful community of artists, musicians, spiritualists, and volunteers.

No one invented money. No one created politics. No one worked for anyone else.

It helped that Inballi came with vast stretches of structures, all free for the taking, with more room than anyone could use in a lifetime. Plus, scattered throughout Inballi, plants grew bearing a wide variety of fast-growing, nutritious, and delicious fruits. Anyone could walk outside their house, pluck a fruit from a nearby plant, and enjoy a wonderful, filling meal.

Thanks to a completely mild climate, clothing was a personal choice, not a matter of survival. A good half of the residents hardly bothered.

Inballi was as close to a lifelong vacation as Eric could imagine. Concerts. Board games. Picnics. Charades. Games of Tag that spanned city blocks. Pets that talked and purred and wagged tails and snuggled. Disease and injury were nonexistent. Aging ceased at the precipice of adulthood.

If anyone ever risked a case of boredom, some creative genius would step in to save the day.

In short, it was the perfect distraction.

Eric and Charlotte faced off against Bob and Sue from across the lawn that separated their houses. Their ongoing game for the past few months involved an overcomplicated game board mowed into the grass they shared. Rules had been negotiated on and off over months, but in the end, the main goal was to join statues in appealing configurations, and where and when those statues moved involved the literal herding of cats to strategically important locations.

While Bob was crouched in a wide stance, barring the passage of a long-haired gray cat toward Eric and Charlotte's territory and Charlotte and Sue made kissy noises vying for the attention of a black-furred kitten, Eric lay in the grass petting an orange tabby he'd coaxed into a scoring zone—the only place petting was allowed. The longer he was able to keep the feline occupied, the greater the score when it finally left.

Meanwhile, in a distant world with no name and no outside residents, another copy of Eric found far more focus.

The school bell rang.

Eric blinked. The world had changed around him. He wasn't outside in the woods, searching for the cause of a wildfire. He was back at his seat. He glanced down at the page in front of him.

IT ALL STARTS HERE

"Drat."

"No talking," Schoolteacher Dad announced on his way in the door, singling Eric out with a wagging finger. "Good morning, class."

"GoOoOd MoOoOrning Mr. RaAaAmsey," the class singsonged back in unison.

"Today, we will be studying Spaceship Crime," Dad announced, tapping out the words in chalk on the green wall slate, barely legible. "Who here can tell me about Spaceship Crime?"

Eric's hand shot up before the class could give their canned answer. "May I use the restroom?" He'd learned many loops ago not to ask if he *could* use the restroom.

Dad lobbed him a plastic paddle with their classroom number on it as a hall pass. "Make it snappy. This is important stuff. Not the kind of thing you'll learn in school and never need again, like Basic Science or How to Say No to Beer."

Eric didn't hesitate. He took the hall pass and booked it down the corridor. He ignored the boys' washroom and ignored the calls from the school administrator—played by Mom—to stop running and get back to class.

He'd managed to hide it all day, but this part of his mind was trapped until he freed it. The rules he'd put in place demanded a solution before any escape. And the only clue he had was that a wildfire starting in the forest outside was going to consume the school.

Find the source.

Put it out.

End the loop.

It wouldn't have been a proper time loop without a calamitous consequence for failure. He needed a tragedy to jar time back to the loop's start. Because he also needed to be able to avert the loop and get out once the solution was set in place.

It would be awful for Dad to survive his capture by the Eyndar Empire only for a loop of Eric's creation to reset and give the rescue another chance to fail.

However, this particular loop may have been too much for a first experiment. He'd lost track of how many recursions he'd experienced. Thousands, by now, he imagined. He'd hated school bells before, and he hated them all the more now. If he'd left this shard of himself with the power to do so, he'd have altered the jarring sound that triggered the loop's restart.

Out in the forest, Eric encountered a wall of fire already too massive to circumvent, roaring toward the school.

No matter how many times he'd tried, he couldn't get out of class and into the forest fast enough to stop the blaze.

This version of Eric was just a boy, not a wizard. He held no power over fire. Gale winds wouldn't blow at his command. Downpours did not await his leave to fall.

Desperate, Eric tried a gambit he hadn't been brave enough to attempt in all his prior journeys through the loop.

Into the flames, he ran, arms upraised to shield his face.

The bell rang, startling Eric as he'd expected to feel more than a rising heat around him. But instead of an agonizing death, he'd ended up back at his desk.

IT ALL STARTS HERE

In stepped Dad with the apple for his desk.

"Good morning, class."

"GoOoOd MoOoOrning Mr. RaAaAmsey," the class singsonged back in unison.

Eric was running out of ideas, and he was trapped in his own personal hell.

Jessie threw off her blanket and sat up.

This was her own bed. She was in her own quarters.

FUCK those were some messed up dreams.

When had she actually fallen asleep? Should she apologize to Hadrian for ditching him?

There was a chime from the door. Checking, Jessie found she was fully dressed, minus the boots by the foot of the bed, and shuffled over to see who was there.

When she opened the door, there was a hover-cart bearing a full English breakfast waiting for her, unattended. Checking up and down the corridor, Jessie couldn't find who'd left it here. But holding a hand above the bacon and eggs, she felt the heat rising and decided that if anyone wanted to play a prank, they'd pay for it later.

After towing the cart inside, Jessie transferred the contents to her table and sat down for a leisurely meal.

A telltale hint of paprika in the scrambled eggs suggested that this was one of Uom'pe's creations, further reassuring Jessie that the mystery meal was legitimate.

Chewing a slice of bacon, Jessie poured herself a coffee, taking a sip before even setting down the carafe with her other hand. She fished out a datapad, scanning for anything that might be urgent and discovering nothing.

Her old, recent comms, just below the new flotsam, didn't stir any recollection. It was all *Arete* business, but she didn't remember issuing these orders, reading these reports that showed up as read, or reviewing the news items that had been forwarded to her.

Relevant? Sure.

The kind of thing they did around here? Yeah.

But did any of it seem like she'd done it yesterday? Not remotely. If anything stirred a memory, it was distant at best.

What *had* she been up to yesterday?

Jessie scanned farther back in her comm history.

Shit.

DAD!

No. That had to be done with by now. She felt no urgency about her father's fate. He must have been set free ages ago, though she didn't recall having anything to do with it.

Or had she?

A headache chose that moment to squeeze her brain through a food processor nozzle.

Memories assailed her. Temple steps and wooden training dummies. Punching a tree until her knuckles bled. Meditating under a waterfall. Practicing kicks with iron weight plates locked around her shins.

It all felt real, as real as anything she'd done in Earth Navy or growing up on the *Mobius*. She remembered the pain, the burning muscles, the gnawing hunger left when a small bowl of rice was her only lunch and half a day's training remained.

But there was more.

Sparring from a handstand position. Meditating *above* a waterfall. Punching a tree until her fist went through. Standing on one leg atop a bamboo pole, shattering boulder after thrown boulder with kicks as fast as a nasty old laaku could pitch them at her.

Her breath started coming quickly.

This was real...

She... vaguely recalled stumbling back to her quarters in the middle of the night for a restful sleep.

Had she spent... decades... in Mortania? In half a night?

Jessie looked down at the tray with her breakfast. Main plate. Side plate. Silverware. Coffee cup. Salt and pepper shakers.

Acting on impulse, she grabbed the tray in both hands and launched the contents toward the vaulted haathee ceiling.

Breakfast scattered into the air. Jessie tossed the tray after it all but with less of an arc.

Her hands moved in a blur. She snatched plates, caught bits of scrambled eggs and bacon and buttered toast and didn't miss a crumb. Silverware she juggled back skyward. The coffee cup snagged on a hooked finger, swooping through the airborne splash of coffee like a vacuum.

With a crash and a clatter, everything landed back on the table. Tray, plates, silverware, and all the rest.

Jessie checked the floor.

She'd missed nothing.

A giddy little chuckle bubbled up inside her.

Pressing pause on breakfast, Jessie tugged off her socks and found a stretch of empty space. It was easy enough in the vast, mostly empty quarters all the human-sized officers lived in.

Taking a deep breath, Jessie tried to calm her nerves. She'd learned to do a tornado kick ages ago. It wasn't the most practical maneuver for military hand-to-hand combat, so she couldn't recall the last time she'd tried one.

But muscle memory, old and new, combined.

"Hop. Spin. Kick," she told herself. Any skilled martial artist could pull one off. She still had the flexibility to kick over head high and the balance to land on her feet. It would be an embarrassing trip to Med Bay if she fucked it up that badly.

Jessie centered herself, bounced on the balls of her feet to prepare, and then...

Hop.

Spin.

Kick-kick-kick-kick-kick-kick.

She landed three meters from her takeoff point, light as a feather.

A grin broke out on her face.

Marching back to the table, she shoveled breakfast down

her throat. Meanwhile, she dismissed a text comm from Harmony with the subject line "URGENT: MASSIVE DRONE FAILURE; SEE ME NOW." Instead, she sent off a text comm of her own.

To: Daphne
Subject: Rematch?

Daphne bit down on her sausage and held the bite between her jaws a moment. Frowning down at her datapad, she reached across the table and showed the message to Mindy.

"Rematch?" Mindy read aloud, incredulous. "What's she want a rematch at? Weren't no match yesterday, tell ya that much. Doc hadn'a stopped ya, you'd have broke her for keeps."

Another chew and a swallow, and Daphne wagged a fork at her lover. "If Dr. Richelieu hadn't kept goading me to push the captain to her limit, she wouldn't have gotten hurt at all."

"'S all this about?" Lisa asked. She was at the next table down in the dining lounge, leaning back in her chair to be nosy. "Something about that dustup in the gym yesterday?"

"Cap'n wants a rematch?" Mindy explained. "You believe that?"

"Must'a rung her bell but good," Lisa agreed. "You gonna do it?"

"No."

The two human women laughed.

"Hell not?" Mindy inquired. "Prob'ly thinkin' she's got her tech sorted. Don't think that was the diff, but hounds aren't horses, eh?"

"Didn't get the knockin' right last time," Lisa added. "Maybe you rough her up good enough, she'll get it in her head that her and Hadrian ain't exactly no cavalry rescue. Her aunt

Tiffany, maybe. Not Hadrian. That one's got it in her for blood when she ain't for fucking. My goddamn hero—don't you dare tell her, neither. We all watched Hadrian get tapped out by the doc, and she's an after-school karate brat."

"Careful," Mindy warned. "Doc's on them drones now, too."

"How's them, anyway?" Lisa asked. "You lot both tryin' 'em, ain'tcha?"

Mindy waved a spoon toward Daphne. "This one's up past four hundred kilos on the weights. Captain wants another piece, she's liable to get herself throwed halfway to the next ship over."

"Excuse-me-but-did-I-hear-that-the-captain-is-considering-another-sparring-bout-with-Lieutenant-Morgan-here?I-only-ask-because-of-my-keen-and-abiding-interest-in-pure-sport-not-because-of-any-financial-stake-I-may-or-may-not-have-had-in-the-prior-contest."

"You bettin' against my girl here?" Mindy asked in mock anger.

"No-no-no-Of-course-not-I-merely-bet-in-favor-of-Captain-Ramsey-There-was-no-betting-*against*-anyone-However-if-there-were-to-be-a-subsequent-rematch-I-would-be-most-interested-in-spreading-the-word-among-the-crew's-more-financially-competitive-members-comfortably-in-advance."

"I don't know about this..." Daphne hedged. "We should check with Dr. Richelieu, at least."

"Yeah. Comm the captain back that you'll do it. I'll round up the spectat—I mean the doc and Britney to make sure it's all safe and whatnot."

———

Jessie hadn't expected word to spread so quickly. By the time she arrived at the self-defense training gym, there was already a crowd of spectators, including Grosstet and Charlotte, not to mention half the ship's Logistics Division.

Daphne was already in a vest and boxing skirt, donning her no-claw gloves so that inadvertent slashes in the heat of the moment didn't kill anyone. Jessie couldn't help but note that she'd forgone that oversized mouthguard that kept her fangs from getting involved—or snapped off.

"You sure you want this?" Daphne asked solemnly.

Jessie stepped onto the mat, and the conversations buzzing throughout the gym died down. "Humor me."

"STOP!" Harmony shouted as she raced in. "What the heck is wrong with you two? Daphne, you have nothing to prove. Your drone enhancements are functioning perfectly. You'd take home a Gold League title with ease if they let you compete. Jessie... do you have any idea how many times you needed your drones yesterday to prevent serious, life-threatening injuries?"

"Thanks for that. I'm good now," Jessie assured her.

Harmony marched up, waving a datapad at her. "Your entire drone network crashed. I can't get a connection to your factories. Not a single drone in your system is responding to commands. Did you let Eric magic you or something?"

"Hadrian showed me some neat tricks."

Harmony pushed up her datagoggles and pinched the bridge of her nose. "Jessie... Jessica. You have *no idea* how much danger you were just in. If you'd started a match without me here or your drones functioning, you could have been killed."

"I'll be fine."

"Yesterday, your drones repaired 16 displaced fractures and generated over 900 milliliters of replacement blood. You'd have been lucky to walk out of here if she'd done it again without a medical team on hand."

"You're here now."

"I'm not sanctioning anything until we get your drone system back online."

Jessie shook her head. "No. I think I'm done fooling with that stuff. Stand back. Daph... let's do this."

The azrin put up her hands. "If the doctor doesn't want us to—"

"No one's hurt yet. She's out of her jurisdiction. Trust me. This is going to be fun."

Reluctantly, Daphne raised her guard and closed in.

Suppressing years of training, Jessie drew on decades of memories from a world that was too real not to exist. Maybe it existed differently, but it was a place. And Master Bentho's teachings applied here, just as well.

She hoped.

Mort had assured her that Mortania was a completely authentic magical domain. He could act outside it if he chose, but otherwise, it was a perfect laboratory for testing magic.

Jessie raised one foot and posed in North Wind Stance.

Trebla heckled from the sidelines. "That shit's make-believe, Jess! You need a stunt suit and camera tricks to pull it off."

This idea of fighting with a Hollyworld stunt suit on had some appeal. Quick reactions from the thrusters *could* replicate certain kip-tie-mahl forms. But a stunt coordinator controlled those thrusters. Getting the same person to fight and run the maneuvering was a pipe dream.

Besides, Jessie didn't need that kind of help.

Daphne's opening jab was a range finder. It fell centimeters short of the mark, and Jessie didn't budge. The follow-up connected with nothing but air. Jessie locked eyes with her opponent and saw the next five attacks coming before the first missed.

Duck.

Twist.

Spin.

Inward block.

Jessie slid beneath one of Daphne's kicks and took her other leg out from under her with a hand sweep.

The crowd was stunned.

Daphne collected herself and rose. "How did you do that?"

"Like I said, Hadrian showed me some tricks."

Over at the edge of the mat, Harmony grunted. "He didn't seem to know any of that last year."

Jessie glanced over, and while he watched from the sidelines, Hadrian The Brown said nothing.

This time around, Jessie went on the offensive.

Open-hand punches.

Lightning-quick kicks.

Daphne made efforts to block or evade, but she might as well have been a wing chun dummy. Jessie moved like wind around her every defense.

Then, a counter-kick caught Jessie in the belly, launching her four meters back.

Jessie landed in a roll and, from a headstand position, spun a 180 and sprang back to her feet, landing in Mountain Thunder Stance.

"They're good tricks, but you're going to get hurt," Daphne warned.

"I didn't want you getting discouraged," Jessie shot back. With a nod, she invited another attack.

Daphne marched forward, emboldened. After all, the "I let you hit me" taunt was almost universally a lie.

Almost.

Daphne threw a punch, and Jessie not only caught it in both hands, she took Daphne's legs out from under her with a shoulder throw. From the ground, the azrin swept a kick that forced Jessie into the air, falling backward into a handstand. Already up and advancing again, the azrin found a whirlwind of kicks as Jessie met her charge from Ocean Over Sky Stance.

Daphne blocked four rotating kicks before dodging back and rolling to gain distance.

Turning her Grain Mill Kicks first into a scissor, then a cartwheel, Jessie returned to upright.

"That looked impractical," Daphne accused. "And you still have no power. You're going to get tired and get yourself hurt."

Dipping into a squat so low that her buttocks nearly hit the mat, Jessie launched herself skyward. With a ceiling just shy of 11 meters, the top of her arc left her within arm's reach. Too impatient for gravity's pull, she shot downward like a bullet, timing a punch for her landing.

Two meters from Daphne, Jessie put her fist through the mat... and the deck plate below.

When she pulled her hand out of the hole, she flexed her fingers to prove that nothing was broken—and her protective glove somehow intact.

"I was pulling all my punches."

The crew gaped.

"I'll be going on the mission. I'll be taking Hadrian with me. The Eyndar Empire has given us our timeline. I want a working insertion and extraction plan in place before they spend a week killing my father. Dismissed."

Harmony lingered as the crew filtered out. "You're not a wizard. I wouldn't rely on magic. It got my mother into as much trouble as it got her out of. Maybe more."

"Understood. Dismissed."

Clearly unappreciative of the dismissal, Harmony nonetheless took the hint and got going.

The only one who'd stuck around in defiance of her "get back to work" implication was Hadrian himself.

"Not a bad show," he admitted. "But you're not ready yet. My belief that you could do it helped more than you might want to know. And still, if she'd had a mind to, Sparta could have thwarted your efforts."

"What about Eric and Charlotte?"

"Eric could have turned you into an actual laaku kip-tie-mahl master mid-fight without you noticing. Charlotte... Maybe you could have done all that despite her efforts."

"So... that's the hierarchy around here? Charlotte, Sparta, Eric, you?"

Hadrian harrumphed. "I bear a grudging respect for the Order of Morpheus, but she's the bottom of their barrel. Sparta's closer to Eric than her. And the three of them together, plus all their friends, are a damp candle if I say so. Which is why I'm confident that I can turn you into enough of a wizard in the scant time available, despite the fact that you're dense as paste."

"Dense?"

"Esper was a competent fighter after a year's training. You took a decade before you could meditate without a solid surface under you. You'll be facing more than a timid azrin on the eyndar homeworld. But I'll have you ready to use your kip-tie-mahl despite angry eyndar wizards and your run-of-the-mill blaster-toting wolves."

Jessie brightened. "Are you telling me I'll be able to do that thing where I bend plasma so it misses me?"

Hadrian's grin was both wicked and conspiratorial. "No,

I'm trying to tell you that when you're ready, you'll be able to *dodge* plasma."

Preparations for the rescue mission kicked into high gear from there.

Days peeled from the calendar amid a flurry of intelligence gathering and planning.

Grosstet oversaw the overhaul of his personal shuttle, conservatively named Shuttle 1. Oh, the adventures this small craft had seen. And what an adventure lay in store for it in the near future.

"Pass the 28 mm wrench, pal of mine?" Jomek asked, patting around the floor with a lower hand in a vain attempt to locate the tool himself. The upper half of the laaku mechanic was wedged solidly inside the eighth lateral maintenance panel of Shuttle 1's passenger compartment. Allowing the *Arete* crew to service the vehicle had taught him that this allowed access to the left-side thrust unit.

Grosstet retrieved a selection of the manual tools and lifted them one by one to eye level, squinting at the tiny human writing on the shaft of each. "AH, HERE WE GO. I COULD RETRIEVE A UNIVERSAL TORQUE ADJUSTER IF YOU LIKE."

The mechanic snatched the wrench away and contorted his body to pass it along to the upper hands, deep within the shuttle's working interior. "Much pass; many thank you. Those things are nearly thirty kilos. Puts my back out just looking at one."

A quick conversion of units in his head confirmed to Grosstet that the laaku's estimate was more or less correct. 28.9 kilograms didn't seem like much—it was just 3 *fruuruu*, after all

—but these tiny sentients and their little muscles demanded delicate tools.

After a few moments of grunting, clangs, and more swears than seemed necessary, Jomek wriggled out from the shuttle's thrust system. "There. Be safe, friend. You're all set for another two months."

"I INTEND TO BE SAFE, HOWEVER I—"

That was when Grosstet caught the laaku patting his shuttle affectionately.

"AH, YOU WERE NOT ADDRESSING ME."

"Sorry to burst your bubble, big boy. You can run your own maintenance just fine."

Grosstet gave him a little toot, not for the words themselves but for the argument they referenced.

Some aboard the *Arete*, in finding out that Grosstet had never done a maintenance overhaul of his shuttle, had declared him to be lucky that he'd never had a major failure. However, when Shuttle 1 ventured upon mission after mission with no incident, now it was somehow thanks to Jomek's fiddling.

Luck had been working just fine.

"How are things going?" the captain asked from the bottom of the open ramp that allowed hangar air and a panoply of scents to pervade the vessel's interior. It wouldn't have been so bad if the peanut smugglers hadn't been sampling their own wares of late; the constant reminders of the delicious little treats made Grosstet's stomach grumble.

"Needs a wax and a blow-dry, but Shuttle 1 is good for rescues."

"I WOULD LIKE TO REITERATE MY OFFER TO PILOT THE MISSION."

Jessie climbed the ramp and looked around. "Duly noted."

Grosstet's ears drooped. "THAT MEANS 'NO.'"

She put a hand on his arm. "I appreciate the offer. I really do. But you'd have to stay with the shuttle, and if we don't get back to the shuttle undetected, I don't think we get back at all. So either we make it and don't need you, or don't make it and you're doomed on the eyndar homeworld in a shuttle with no star-drive."

Jomek piped up. "Not putting a star-drive in here. Don't know the systems well enough. Don't want to vouch for it working if I did."

"It's a one-shot mission. No do-overs. I only want known, reliable equipment for this one," Jessie informed the pair.

As she headed out of earshot, Jomek lowered his voice. "And yet, she still picks Hadrian as her muscle."

"MUCH CONFUSION; MANY ANNOYANCE."

"It's all so horrible," Mom declared, as if Harmony needed to be told. "I may have had my differences with Carl, but... this is awful."

Yes, Mom, it's both horrible and awful. Harmony could see why she'd employed speech writers.

"I can't let you in on the details, but we've got something in the works to get him back. How are Mom and the girls?"

It was weird referring to her little sisters as "the girls" since they were all grown adults now, but old habits died hard. They had no other collective term in her mind.

"Oh, you know how they are. Summer went full-on activist mode about the Ghenlar Par'Mol situation. Grace is thinking about going back to school for interstellar policy. Nobody's admitted to being pregnant, though Autumn swears she's trying. Probably not as hard as Minuet... but I'm not judging."

Sure you're not, Mom.

"How's Mom?"

"Working. She's starting up with a Poltid Tourism Ministry campaign to infuse human money into the economy."

"Is the Tourism Ministry still just Donu and Mordo?"

"No. They added an accountant, on account of them not being any good with a budget. Your mother's working pro bono as a favor to Kubu."

Harmony forced a smile. She wished she could be there with the family on Poltid. She also wished Britney hadn't informed her of this comm as she was walking past her own office. The polite way to deal with a comm from your boss's mother wasn't to chitchat with her until the boss came back.

"I should really be going, Mom. It's been good catching up."

"I understand. Duty calls."

"Exactly."

"I just want you to know, if I were twenty years younger..."

"I get it, Mom. I know. We'll figure out a way to bring him home."

"Bye, babycheeks."

"Bye, Mom." Harmony held a smile and a wave in place until the connection closed, then slumped. "Medic Daschel?"

Britney appeared in the doorway with a dopey grin on her face. "Doctor?"

"Don't do that again?"

"Aw. Your mom's bonzer. I'll trade you for mine and talk to her every day till she's sick of me."

Harmony supposed she *did* have a pretty bonzer pair of mothers. But that wasn't the point. Busy schedule aside, there was still the matter of a chain of command. "Put me on the spot like that again, and I'll demote you to Logistics Division."

"I'd be a star," Britney replied without missing a beat. "Reach two levels of shelving without the sleds? I'd be queen of levels 2 and 3."

"I'm serious."

"Don't take it wrong, Doctor, but you can bust me down to private and put a rifle in my hands again. I won't stop looking out for you. Talking to your mom's good for the noggin. Keeps you grounded."

Without a strong counterargument, she pulled rank. "Just get back to work."

The grin didn't budge. "Of course, Doctor."

Britney was angling to be around for the long haul, that was for certain. She didn't look forward to the discussion with Mom if she fired her.

━━━

Eric sobbed.

His tears wet the sheet of paper on his desk.

IT ALL STARTS HERE

Schoolteacher Dad allowed the spectacle on the grounds of "crying is just one of those things."

Every few loops had become a Crying Loop. A good long cry in frustration and hopelessness, allowing the fire to consume the school unimpeded, gave him enough emotional *oomph* to get through a few more tries.

"Today, we will be studying Spaceship Crime. Who here can tell me about Spaceship Crime?"

"We don't knoOooOw anything about SpaAaAceship Criiiime." Eric mouthed the words in flawless unison with the other students.

"Correct. But also, there's more to it than that. You see, part of crime—the most *important* part—is not getting caught. Who can come up with a way not to get caught doing Spaceship Crimes?"

Eric just wanted to *do* some spaceship crimes.

Why had the main Eric not rescued him by now? What could he possibly gain from putting this fraction of himself through this kind of torment? He wasn't figuring it out. What was the point of keeping him here?

Unless Big Eric had forgotten him.

Or decided to permanently abandon him to this fate. There would be no emotional trauma either way. The only risk to Big Eric was Magic-Free Eric returning emptyhanded and emotionally devastated.

He *had* to get out of here.

The schoolroom chatter blathered on in the background until the flames rose.

The Bell rang.

"Good morning, class."

"GoOoOd MoOoOrning Mr. RaAaAmsey," the class singsonged back in unison.

IT ALL STARTS HERE, the paper said.

Eric mashed a hand down on the page and crumpled it into a ball. Without waiting for leave, he sprang from his desk and ran the length of the room. To the window. Out the window. Previous attempts to leave via the window had been thwarted by a sticky twist-lock mechanism that took a few tries to work loose. The climb down from the window lost him time as well.

Like a holovid action hero—admittedly, probably not as skillfully—he crashed through a shattering of glass.

Pain.

Blood.

Broken bits of glass.

Terrified both of the coming flames and of the gushing loss of blood, Eric scrambled to his feet and rushed into the forest.

There was no fire.

Not yet.

If he could just get to the source. Maybe he could finally stop it.

Reckless campers?

A technology device going haywire?

Kids playing with matches? Eric hadn't even seen a match in real life, but his imagination knew they were a forest fire waiting to happen.

Goodness, was he dripping a lot of...

... blood.

Dizzy after only a few dozen steps, Eric collapsed to the forest floor.

Overhead, a reddish beam flashed across the sky.

No. Not the sky. Below the canopy of leaves above him.

Struggling to sit up, he managed to see the source: the rooftop of the school.

Fires roared. Eric could barely keep his eyes open, let alone stand. Let even *more* alone run.

The Bell rang.

"Good morning, class."

"GoOoOd MoOoOrning Mr. RaAaAmsey," the class singsonged back in unison.

IT ALL STARTS HERE, the paper reminded him.

You sneaky paper! You were telling me the answer all along!

Eric was above this kind of underhanded misdirection. That's why he both knew he wouldn't fall for it and most definitely *had*.

It took eight more loops before Eric managed to reach the rooftop before the flames rose and restarted everything.

His most obvious attempt had been a locked door labeled Roof Access. But as a non-wizard and no physical specimen, that door might as well have been a wall.

A stepladder in the janitor's closet was a slow and

cumbersome process, and he ran out of time before even managing to set it up outside the school.

Multiple iterations got Eric the information about where to find the key, then distract the janitor into leaving it unattended. Once all *that* was worked out, Eric managed to unlock the door on a clean attempt the next loop.

Atop the roof was a scene he never expected.

Uncle Roddy was there, dressed in a scientist's lab coat, overseeing a folding table piled with rickety contraptions. Wires and cables, mirrors and lenses.

Eric arrived just in time to watch the flipping of a big, clunky mad-scientist switch.

"Gah!" Uncle Roddy exclaimed as the machine went crazy. Mirrors tilted akimbo. Sparks lightninged around.

A beam of red laser zorched out into the dry underbrush of the nearby forest.

"What are you doing, Uncle Roddy?" Eric demanded. "Why did the machine go *kerplunk*?"

The laaku in the lab coat whirled on him. "That's *Mr. Rodek*, young man! And I do believe it was more of a *kerplooie*."

"You set the forest on fire!"

"I did no such thing. I merely—Oh. Oh shit. You're right. This isn't good. No, not good at all."

"How do we stop it?"

"Stop it? It's too late."

"It can't be too late! We have to—where are you going?"

Eric raced after the laaku as he waddled toward the door back down to ground level, arms laden with scientific equipment.

"Anywhere but here!"

Not that it mattered, the fires roared up and surrounded the school. It annoyed Eric anew that it was apparently *entirely surrounded* by the dry, flammable forest. How did anyone even get here? Was there a road he'd yet to discover?

It didn't matter how these fictional people got to school each day. Eric knew exactly how.

The Bell rang.

"Good morning, class."

"GoOoOd MoOoOrning Mr. RaAaAmsey," the class singsonged back in unison.

IT ALL STARTS HERE.

It's all going to end here, too.

Two more loops had been sufficient for Eric to decide that finding the key to the rooftop door was too slow.

The next time around, as soon as Schoolteacher Dad set the apple down on his desk, Eric ran up and snatched it away.

"Hey! Put that back. Snack time isn't until second period. And besides, that's mine. Get your own apple!"

Eric ignored the scolding. He'd gotten enough practice in childhood that Dad's admonitions were raindrops against Eric's umbrella of indifference.

Though never athletic, even a dope like him could hit a target at point-blank range. Eric pitched the firm, fresh-picked fruit through the glass of the classroom's window. Cringing at the looming shard still clinging to the window frame, Eric stuck his head out and looked up.

"MISTER RODEK! DON'T TURN ON THE MACHINE. IT'S GOING TO GO KERPLOOIE!"

Eric waited.

There was no beam of light. Instead, a laaku head poked over the ledge. "What's this all about?"

A soul-weary sigh of relief escaped Eric. "Let me up there and I'll explain everything. Oh. And maybe smooth things over with Mr. Ramsey for me..."

Eric's eyes snapped open. Which was a good trick since they'd been open already. "Aha!"

"Aha, what?" Charlotte inquired. She tapped at a datapad, painstakingly with one finger, as Eric loitered in her office between her appointments.

"I, uh, guess I need a snack."

Charlotte glanced up. "I have an appointment in six minutes. I can't gallivant, presently."

"Want me to bring you back something? Maybe something that won't get cold or dry or melty if it has to wait? Or unmelty, if it's cheese-based."

"I'm fine, thank you. Enjoy your treat."

Eric wondered what he'd get himself.

The whole ride down the lift toward the dining lounge, he was a ball of jitters.

His experiment had worked.

He felt awful for how long he'd been trapped in that time loop. That's what he got for pitting fragments of his mind against one another. He knew his own blind spots and the blind spots to his blind spots. If anyone was qualified to give Eric Ramsey absolute fits, it was another Eric Ramsey.

But that didn't matter now because it had worked.

It had *worked*.

Maybe the real world didn't work like his imagination imagined. But he'd put in so much effort to recreating a reality-neutral magical environment. He had to imagine that his imagination was right. If he hadn't, he couldn't. And if he couldn't, he wouldn't ever again.

The recursive thoughts were hurting even his head, and he spent a *lot* of time contemplating temporal conundrums.

"What. Can I. Get you?" a chipper Uom'pe asked as he entered her domain.

Eric gave careful consideration. If anything went wrong with his father's rescue, and he needed to trigger the loop, he could be eating this between-meal meal quite a bit. Nothing finicky. Nothing experimental. There were enough variables here already. Eric needed a tried-and-true crowd pleaser.

"Strawberry pancakes with butter and syrup, please," Eric replied with a pleasant grin.

He took a seat and waited.

In his head, he ran through the logical trap he'd employed in his mind.

In the true timeline, my father doesn't die in the Eyndar Empire. If Carl Ramsey were to die, that would prove that the timeline was wrong.

Uom'pe delivered his pancakes.

Eric took a deep sniff, closing his eyes a moment before thanking the tesud.

As Uom'pe retreated to the kitchen, Eric took his fork and held it at arm's length.

Here goes nothing...

The fork fell with a clatter that rang through the dining lounge.

IT ALL STARTS HERE

———

Among the many perks of sharing private quarters and having negligible responsibilities aboard a starship was how quickly playfully feeding one another bites of lunch could turn into foreplay.

A trail of discarded garments led from the kitchen table to

Hadrian and Sparta's bed. Pawing and groping atop the rumpled sheets, he wore nothing but his Convocation medallion. Sparta kept hers on in addition to her copious jewelry.

Despite the numerous other uses of mouths, they managed to carry on a civil conversation.

"I'm actually taking a liking... to native tesud cuisine," Sparta said.

"That's fine... as far as it goes... but you get sick of salads after a while. And once you... mmm... realize that everything is a salad of one sort of another, the novelty loses... its shine."

"Surely. Just... I think I could... ohhhh... see it becoming a staple. Somewhat like... tacos or... mmmm... pizza."

Hadrian grunted. With Sparta spread atop him, he was less inclined than usual to argue minutiae. "Fair enough. Just... let's see... about how often we eat salad."

"I could definitely—" Sparta's whole body stiffened, and Hadrian couldn't think of anything specific he'd done to elicit that reaction. She was even holding her breath.

"If you need me to move my fingers, I can certainly—"

"Shush," she scolded. "Don't move." The spell passed, and her features relaxed. "That was just the most intense feeling of déjà vu."

"Didn't think I was being that repetitive."

Sparta shook her head, raining a few droplets of sweat. She took a heaving breath. "No. It's not your fault. I don't know what it was other than distracting."

"Can you describe it?"

"If normal déjà vu is someone shouting your name, this is everyone jumping out from behind the furniture to surprise you with a birthday party."

"My family didn't do those after Grandpa Nebuchadnezzar's hundredth birthday resulted in three funerals. Surprising a Guardian of the Plundered Tomes is bad mojo."

"Well, I'd like one very specific form of distraction, if you don't mind. Hadrian, could you be a darling and squelch my magic?"

"I thought you hated that."

"Granted. But what I've discovered I hate even more is feeling an oncoming climax and having it slapped aside by my premonitions. Make a game of it. Get on top of me, smother my magic, pin me with your own if you like, and do whatever you like with me."

Hadrian smirked. "Letting you have your way *is* what I like. Call it the privilege of power."

Sparta rolled off him and tugged him by the wrist to switch places. "Hadrian. This is a favor. I'm not often overwhelmed by my foresight. I just need someone to shut the lights off and lead me out of it by the hand. So stop being a studly gentleman for a while and just become a rakish cad. For me. Please?"

"Are you sure?"

"Hear my 'yes' and pretend that I said 'no' and that you didn't care."

"Whatever you say."

Sparta growled playfully. "You're incorrigible!"

———

Half of Trebla's test lab had been cordoned off to foot traffic. Not that he got a lot of visitors, but an experimental engineer couldn't be too careful. As an additional safety precaution, he'd built himself a bunker as well. In lieu of sandbags, he had stacked giant sacks of canine anti-dander powder pillaged from Eyndar Outpost 71 that no one had found any other use for.

Even Daphne had done some omni research and concluded that the stuff would play hell on her skin.

Secretly, Trebla liked the smell of the stuff. But he had his own fur-care routine, and this stuff was the equivalent of taking home urinal cakes to clean your dishes.

Right now, all he cared about was that 2.8 tons of the stuff should dissipate a wild ricochet from an eyndar standard-issue military blaster rifle.

Downrange, in the empty half of the lab, was a slab of scrap steel tinted with a target. Just the far side of the bunker, barely out of arm's reach, an inexpertly welded framework clamped the aforementioned eyndar blaster rifle firmly in place.

Perched atop the stacks of anti-dander powder, a holocam watched as Trebla triggered the blaster rifle on remote.

Hot red plasma lashed out on full power from the rifle.

However, the rifle wasn't sighted on the target. Instead, it struck a custom glove Trebla had put together from small sections of the *Arete's* hull. The gloves themselves were standard military fare, straight off the hands of some dead pirate or another who wore the right size for his purposes and given a thorough cleaning.

The modification had been of the backing plates. The alloy was akin to mulberry, heavy on uranium and mixed with niobium, zirconium, and an isotope of tantalum he couldn't reproduce. Thanks to the dense metal, each glove was more than two kilos.

In theory, while inconvenient to the wearer, the extra mass would land a harder punch, but that was hardly the gloves' intended function.

Trebla had accounted for ricochets in his safety plan because that was the whole idea.

Activating the remote, the *Arete's* chief engineer fired.

In realtime, all Trebla saw on the holo feed was a crooked

afterimage of red. Slowing the playback, he watched the plasma jet out from the rifle's barrel, strike the glove he'd mounted, and reflect the blast in the direction of the tinted target.

Trebla missed by 8 cm, but that wasn't the point. His haste in setting up the experiment had been a necessity. The idea for this kind of protective wear had been in the back of his mind for months, but when Jessie had requested anything he could come up with on short notice, he'd compressed his timeline with hydraulic efficiency.

A second shot followed the first and struck the same spot.

So did the third.

And the fourth.

By the fifth shot into the same growing hole in his scrap piece, Trebla worried for the safety of his wall. The interior of the *Arete* wasn't made of blaster-reflective material.

First shutting off the blaster remotely, then exiting his bunker to remove the power pack and discharge the single shot remaining in the pre-ignition chamber, Trebla headed down to see how his glove had fared.

The only marks on the glove were a carbonic residue from impurities in the eyndar-manufactured power pack. A wipe from his sleeve, and the pale purplish uranium alloy was smooth and unblemished.

Whipping out his datapad, he fired off a comm to Jessie.

They're ready.

Meditation using a candle to help the mind clear itself of distractions was a time-honored method. Jessie's modern version used an image of a candle on a datapad she sandwiched between two stiff, flattened palms.

Not only did she have to ignore outside distractions, but the datapad itself popped up frequent reminders of upcoming appointments and incoming messages. Plus, she kept her TeleJack on. There was a setting so that in proximity to her active datapad, the thing wouldn't duplicate alerts, but she'd shut off that feature. The more distractions, the better the training to block them out.

But this one, she'd been waiting for.

They're ready, said Trebla's text comm.

Allowing her concentration to lapse, Jessie fell.

The sensation of freefall no longer upset her inner ear. Gravity existed for her as needed. From a cross-legged position, she kicked out her legs in a split as she somersaulted backward before aligning one beneath her for a landing.

Casually drawing herself upright, she opened Trebla's message, but the subject line was the totality of its contents.

The TeleJack and datapad both appeared to be in good working order. In the two weeks she'd been working on this exercise, it had only been in the last three days that they'd both come through fully functional. Part of it had been overcoming her instinctive fear of the 3-meter fall from a relaxed position.

Admitting to Harmony days later that her first fall had resulted in a cracked hip hadn't won her any awards for toughness down in Med Bay, but it *had* confirmed—to the doctor's dismay—that her body had broken down and eliminated all traces of the H-tech drones and factories for making more.

Jessie no longer gorged herself on seven meals a day. In fact, she barely ate.

She promised herself a celebratory beer with Dad when they got him back, but she hadn't touched a drink since training in Mortania began.

Two weeks...

Time passed strangely in there, even for passing strangely compared to the outside world. Days could last weeks and nights were mere blips for a little stargazing before dawn raced up and took over. But to call her stays decades might have been a low estimate.

And each time, Jessie started anew.

Master Bentho pretended not to remember her. Techniques she'd mastered had to be relearned from scratch. She endured the same hazing, the same journey of discovery, the same hammering into a weapon that defied both gravity and limitations of the flesh.

Each cycle, she was more of a prodigy. In exchange for greater promise and potential, Master Bentho was commensurately harder on her.

As she made her way to the lift barefoot, in a loose t-shirt and baggy slacks, Jessie reviewed the other comms she'd ignored for the past six hours. Intel reports, status updates, refinements to maps they'd been collecting and cross-checking from multiple sources.

They'd had a saying when she was growing up on the *Mobius*, with its notorious single washroom: shit or pass the turn. Felt appropriate now, given the originator of the phrase was their target. But Dad would have agreed. If things in Trebla's lab measured up, it would be time for the decorative frosting and to light the candles on this mission.

When she arrived at the lab, Trebla practically threw the gloves at her.

"Try them on. Let me know if they're too heavy. I think I might be able to grind down some pebbles and see if Hadrian can turn them into—"

"Seem fine," Jessie declared. The gloves had slipped right on and cinched at the wrist. She'd picked them out herself and once again silently thanked the pirate with the missing front teeth for being exactly her size. "I can get used to the heft."

A few quick taps, and she sent a message from her datapad.

Security alert. Intruder in engineering lab. This is a drill.

In under a minute, Lisa, Daphne, and Mindy had all arrived, blasters at the ready.

Jessie strolled onto the firing range. "Minimum power, just in case."

"Just watch the angle on those," Trebla warned. "I haven't done extensive testing on high-impact-angle shots."

Her three security officers took up positions in Trebla's bunker like colonial rebels about to repel oncoming marines.

Jessie measured her breathing.

Plasma flew.

She didn't react; she preacted. Even to her own eyes, Jessie's hands became a blur.

But in a state of heightened awareness, she discovered so much more. Trebla's winces, worried about the safety of his lab equipment. Lisa's frustration. Mindy's eyes widening with awe. Daphne slightly turned on, pupils otherwise too wide for the well-lit lab.

No plasma touched her. Every shot deflected to Trebla's designated backstop despite it being more work than simply protecting herself.

She stepped to her right. Now her body blocked the target from the shooters. "Hit the target."

With the trio taking renewed aim, Mindy voiced a question. "We getting scored on accuracy or just not hitting you?"

"Try for the bullseye, but I'm not keeping score." Then, taking up Twin Willow Stance, she resolved not to move her feet.

Shots flew.

Jessie contorted. She twisted. She bent backward until her hair brushed the floor. Clinging to the sole thought of keeping her feet planted, she became a turnstile for the hail of plasma zipping past her.

"Switch to stun. Don't mind the walls. Anyone who can hit me gets a promotion."

"I'm in!" That was enough for Trebla to unmount the test rifle from its moorings and swap to nonlethal fire.

The stun blasts were less focused. Bigger. Harder to dodge.

But Jessie also relieved herself of the requirement to remain planted on the floor.

Hop.

Roll.

Spring.

Her security officers and chief engineer worked in concert —though Trebla wasn't as adept at the Security Division's teamwork. They tried to lead her into one another's firing line. They anticipated her movements.

Jessie anticipated right back at them.

Not only that, she reacted to shots already in the air. Though it hardly mattered under normal combat circumstances, the stun energy did travel slower. Jessie moved like a hummingbird charged with lightning.

"If you're doing this with a holo-projector," Trebla called out, "I'm calling it right now: prank of the year."

Jessie ran up the walls, sprang off the ceiling, shifted momentum in midair to avoid what ought to have been sure hits.

Then, what must have appeared impossible to the shooters, she charged. One second, she was gliding in at the zenith of an arcing jump, 2 meters from the lab's ceiling, the next, her personal, internal gravity shot her toward the bunker of veterinary-care sacks.

Twice along the twenty meters or so she had to travel, Jessie altered her definition of "down" to avoid running into oncoming fire. She struck the sacks with enough force to topple the pile. In the resulting scramble, she wrested Lisa's weapon from her hands.

Daphne fired a panicked shot, stunning Mindy. Trebla's aim was better, but his own reflexes failed him as Jessie realigned the barrel to point at Daphne before he squeezed the trigger. His own weapon came away easily with a quick tug.

"I surrender!" her laaku cousin exclaimed, dropping to the ground and covering up.

Jessie addressed her acting security chief, the only one still standing beside her. "Final mission briefing at 1500 hours. Time to light the fuse. I'm sure Harmony will be by any second to wonder why these two short-circuited." She bent down. "As for you, tough guy, don't pick up a blaster if you don't want to play. Make yourself useful and round up Hadrian, let him know about the briefing. He ought to sit in on this one, at least."

"Yes, ma'am," Trebla squeaked without unballing.

"Oh, get up. You're fine. And... thanks for the gloves. They work great."

<hr>

After a quick dusting off of his fur and an even quicker change of personal wear, Trebla hustled across the ship in search of Hadrian. The wizard's refusal to carry a datapad was understandable. After all, in all the years he'd known Uncle Enzio, he hadn't seen the guy use one except as a coaster or as a prop to level a corner of that ratty old couch in the *Mobius* common room. But his reluctance to be on constant vigil in his quarters for someone to come looking for him was all the more vexing because of the datapad thing.

It had become a running gag.

"You seen Hadrian?" "Sure, lots of times..."

It wasn't funny the first time, and it didn't get funnier with repetition. Except from Uom'pe. Somehow, her glacial delivery was the right comedic timing.

"Indeed. I. Have. He's. In. Here often." Just struck the right nerve and still made Trebla chuckle despite his growing annoyance.

Eventually, he discovered the ship's youngest wizard in the Room of Runes, or The Sandbox, or whatever people wanted to call it. Until someone pulled the trigger on tinting it on the doors, any name would remain unofficial.

"Didn't think I'd find you here," he admitted as he approached the wizard, slipping off his walking gloves before getting them sandy. "Whatcha doing over there?"

"Oh, just finishing up a side project."

"Does Eric know you're messing with his astral drop setup?" Trebla asked, mildly worried about their next transit all of a sudden.

Hadrian scoffed. "For every grain of sand on this floor, there are a hundred things Eric doesn't know. Some he should but doesn't. Others he should be grateful about. And believe me"—he gave a nod toward Trebla's walking gloves—"he's got plenty of sand in his shoes."

"OK. I'm good on the fortune cookies, bud. Just here to pull you in on the 3 p.m. clansmoot in ye olde Briefing Room."

Rather than take offense at the ribbing, Hadrian harrumphed. "About time."

Trebla couldn't put a finger on it, but something had been bothering him. "Why's this such a big deal to you? I mean... I've known Carl my whole life, and I'd have second thoughts going on this one. Eric could have handled the astral business. He keeps his shit together pretty good when it's about to hit the blowers. Jess can handle the eyndar. I don't care if it's an army. I just saw her showing off her kip-tie-mahl with the new plasma-reflective gloves I built her. It'd take at least three armies to slow her down."

A sad little smirk curled the wizard's lip. "She's the pilot. If I could fly a ship myself, I'd go alone. But I need someone reliable to get me to Here We Live or however you want to translate that nonsense lack of a name of their homeworld. And I can worry a little *less* now that she can handle herself with magic instead of tech."

"You're not worried she'll forget how to fly?"

"Tiffany barely had her learner's license and still knows how to get around the galaxy."

Trebla perked up. "You've met her?"

Hadrian stood impassive.

"What's with the mystery-man bit? It was a simple enough question."

"Ask a harder one, Trebla. You know you've been wanting to."

Bile rose in the back of Trebla's throat. "I'm not sure I want to."

"All the more reason to ask."

Trebla shook his head and started backing toward the door. "Message delivered. I'm good. Have a safe trip."

With a snap of his fingers, a tornado filled the Room of Runes. Sand blew toward the walls, rising until the sand itself *was* a wall. The circular chamber cleared of all floorbound debris until the metal showed clearly.

At first, Trebla had figured it was merely a bit of assholish magic to keep him from leaving before receiving permission. Then, he realized it was *also* meant to reveal Hadrian's side project.

Over the wind's howl, the wizard raised his voice. "These

runes are top of the line. Best work I've done in years—at least on anything bigger than a necklace. Sparta or even Charlotte ought to be able to use this glyph to get the *Arete* in and out of astral without the need of fancy contraptions."

"I... recognize these."

It had been a while. Aunt Amy hated manual astral travel. But on the rare occasions when their star-drive on the *Mobius* was busted, Uncle Enzio busted out the runes that ringed the common room floor and did it himself.

These same runes.

"Y-y-you're not, by any chance, Enzio Stiles in disguise?"

"Enzio wasn't the one who etched the floor of the *Mobius*."

Trebla gulped. He shook his head.

"Go ahead. Say it. It's all right."

"(Mort?)"

Hadrian cupped a hand to his ear. "Huh? What?"

"Mordecai The Brown."

Hadrian smiled. "Been too long."

"What happened to Hadrian? Is... Have you always... I'm... But why now?"

"Hadrian's fine. Happy, even. Got him a cushy gig. As for why now? Because I'm about to do something stupid and dangerous, and believe it or not, hiding my identity is a slight hindrance to my power. Jessica knows. Eric's known too long for his own good. Charlotte's probably wormed it out of Eric by now, and I told Sparta before we got serious. I'm letting the air out of this balloon slowly, so don't go blabbing. Cat's not entirely out of the bag, but there are enough holes that I'm hearing whispers about whiskers behind my back. I don't know how long I'll keep up the charade, but I'll take one technologist's belief in magic with me on this mission for good luck.

"Do you believe, Trebla?"

Trebla nodded as if his life depended on it.

"Merlin's beard, kid," Hadrian huffed. "If I didn't kill your father a hundred different times, you've sure as hell got nothing to worry about. Now... you said I've got a meeting at... 1500 hours they'd call it?"

"Yeah. Yes. I mean, yes, *sir*."

"Fuck's sake, aren't you a commander or some bullshit in Jessie's little private navy? Show some backbone and stop calling me sir this instant."

"Yes, sir."

The sandstorm swirled to a halt, leaving an atoll in a sea of steel with the rune circle mostly still exposed.

"That's more like it. Now, what bloody time is it?"

Trebla pulled out a datapad. "It's, uh, 1305 right now." As he turned his wrist to check, however, a river of tiny granules poured out from the walking gloves.

He left the Room of Runes barehanded.

━━━

Jessie took the seat just left of the head of the table in the Briefing Room. She was the subject of this mission review, not the presenter. Out of uniform, she was clad all in tactical-grade matte black. A quick visit to Jomek behind Trebla's back had even tinted the garish purple of the reflector gloves to match, plus, he'd cut the fingertips off the gloves for her at just the right spot.

After leaving Trebla's lab and dropping off the gloves with his top mechanic, Jessie had gone back to her quarters in a state of weirdly calm clarity.

She'd cut her own hair, laser-shaved her legs and underarms, and taken a shower and a nap.

There was often time for a meal during a long mission. For

multi-day missions, it was all but a necessity. Sleep, you'd catch that here and there if you had platoonmates to watch over you.

But there never seemed to be time enough to get *clean*. The feeling of fresh, soap-cleansed skin and clothes that weren't holding in sweat and blood and grit and grime. That came later. Going into a mission, if she had the chance, Jessie always liked to freshen up.

Now, it was like hearing another world echoing in from her past.

She'd seen iterations of this plan a hundred times as it evolved.

She'd seen it a thousand more in her dreams.

Jessie sipped her coffee and watched the final version unfold in a clinical, pristine form that would never actually exist, no matter how hard they tried.

On the Briefing Room holo, an Earth-like appeared. Most of them were gorgeous blue-green paradises like Keru or even Meyang. Some had become glistening ultra-modern marvels in the vein of Earth or Phabian. But this one was sickly and drab, a barren biome of rock and dirt, long since strip-mined to worthlessness, surrounded by clouds. The surface was gloomy, hot, and basically in a constant state of counter-terraforming to maintain a semblance of habitability.

Lisa held out an upturned hand toward it. "This is the Eyndar Empire homeworld. Earth-like in name only. Rotten doggos gone and wrecked it up something awful. Capital city, Imand'Vol, is roundabout where Copenhagen Prime oughtta be."

The holographic map zoomed in, breaking cloud cover and centering on the European Region before continuing into the Denmark District and beyond.

City streets resolved as a network of irregular connections, casting the city "blocks" in a variety of nonstandard shapes.

Something one might expect more of a toddler with safety scissors and plastisheet than the works of paid city architects.

"This here mess is what they call a city. An' I don't want a word out of you wizzies that it ain't no worse than Earth. It is."

Without pausing her sip of coffee, Jessie intervened, leaning in and tapping to advance the presentation. Multiple locations in the green-scale wireframe turned red.

Lisa cleared her throat and pointed. "Right oh. That there's the prison where Carl's cooped up. We got him on newsfeeds mentions ten times a day with up-to-date calendar countdown and whatnot. They ain't done him in once yet or they'd be rioting for not seein' it firsthand. They's still fer flapping their jowls off, cryin' about pups he murdered and similar rubbish.

"The other shite I got in red here is the imperial palace, the military headquarters, and the clubhouse of their take on a Convocation."

Hadrian harrumphed softly. "At least Earth had the good sense to separate the meat brains and magicrats on separate continents."

"Gonna start with the good news," Lisa continued. "This here's a festival in the middle of summer. Gonna be loads of strangers in town, loaded up in cool-suits and breather masks. Most of the locals can take the air quality bein' 750 parts per million. Special injections and implants and all that. Offworld visitors, not so much. We got a pair of cool-suits and snout-masks with goggles to keep the doggos from catchin' on right off."

No one brought up the scent issue. Not after the last several meetings. The rancid outdoor odors kept most of the eyndar populace scent-blind on their homeworld.

"That ends the good news. Now for the bad. You lot are going to perform a blind suborbital, subterranean astral drop from the nosebleed astral straight down this here sewer main."

The image zoomed once more, burrowing the Briefing Room's view through solid rock and underground not far from the prison.

"Assuming you survive, on account of the rest of this plan don't do a whole lot if you push daisies halfway to getting there, you'll head out through the cleansing station and across a couple streets to the prison. Ain't no direct route in pipes on account of the doggos is too dumb to rebuild a thousand-year-old prison with modern plumbing. You'll sneak as far into the prison as you can get"—the view moved slowly, trailing a proposed path deemed "optimal," while Jessie could only see a dozen variants based on circumstances they would encounter—"then you fight the rest of the way, grab Carl, and skedaddle back out. Easy peasy."

There were a few nervous laughs around the briefing table.

"Not a laughing matter," Hadrian pointed out. "The hard part will be getting to Carl before those eyndar get the yips. I lay eyes on him, it's clear sailing through bloody waters."

Even Jessie, zen-like in her pre-mission state of detachment, couldn't help a chill running up her spine. She'd known Enzio Stiles since birth. He was a lazy clod, told funny stories, and generally kept out from underfoot as Dad's band gallivanted across the galaxy. Here or there, he would chip in with a warning about a bad situation, and the *Mobius* would abandon a gig and hit the stars. She wondered now, looking back, how many of those situations were a missing person who might be traced back to them? How many times had there been a magical battle concealed from the kids?

Uncle Enzio was the sheep's clothing to hide Dad's old mass-murdering friend in retirement.

Hadrian was peeking out from beneath the wool with very old eyes, all of a sudden.

Lisa continued onward, delving into details of parade

routes, civil defense patrols, and known identities of prison guards. At any point, one of the officers on her planning team or her partner for this mission could have raised an objection, requested clarification, or given a reason anew why this whole operation was suicide.

Too many unknown variables.

Dad not being worth the risk.

Astral charts not being accurate enough for their arrival target.

Astral travel within a gravity well, atmosphere, or structure being contraindicated by every authority on the subject except the one in the briefing room with them.

But no one stopped the meeting.

Jessie issued a dismissal. Officers filtered out, subdued, all knowing that their part was done and there was little else but worrying ahead of them.

Hadrian spared a hint of a nod as he exited, presumably to comfort or seek comfort from Sparta.

Charlotte lingered. "A word, before you depart?"

"Go ahead. You're as good as in command already."

"It's about your brother," the wizard continued, and Jessie couldn't be sure now whether this was going to be a conversation with Commander Webber, Wizard Charlotte, or the woman who was quickly becoming family in her own right.

"You handle him better than I do, these days. What's the problem with him?"

"He's been acting strangely."

Jessie laughed. The humor came as a welcome valve on the stress building inside her. "Please tell me this isn't the first time you noticed."

"Strangely given his baseline idiosyncrasies. Just the past two days or so. He's squirreling all over the ship, bothering everyone about odd details of their involvement in the rescue efforts."

Jessie scowled. "You're not suggesting..."

"I'd have Hadrian check thoroughly for stowaways if we don't have Eric on hand and within line of sight when you depart."

Fuck. She wanted to argue. But it seemed plausible enough. "I'd like to think Eric wouldn't be stupid enough to try that, but—"

"Hey!" an offended voice objected from beneath the conference table. "Oops!"

Jessie and Charlotte both crouched and bent and found the aforementioned out-of-sorts wizard sitting with his knees hugged to his chest, where presumably he'd hidden the entire length of the briefing.

"You're not coming."

Eric shook his head emphatically. "Wouldn't dream of it. Just trying to learn everything I can. You know. Bits and pieces. In case..."

"In case what?" Jessie asked, weary now before the mission even began.

"In case something goes wrong and I need to help."

"Nothing's going to go wrong. Nothing we can't handle," Jessie promised.

Charlotte lent her support. "Hadrian has grown markedly over his final year at Oxford. He's as formidable as his heritage would have suggested. And Jessie can more than take care of herself. You won't be asked to do anything. I promise."

"Same," Jessie confirmed. "Just sit back, maybe put in a good word with the universe, and wait for us to get back with Dad. OK?"

"OK." Eric's voice was tiny. "But, you know... if something goes wrong..."

Carl was starting to get used to his prison cell. When the door clanged shut behind him, it came as something of a relief. Twelve hours was a long time to stand with his feet shackled to the base of a podium as widow after orphan after comrade-in-arms told stories of the friends and loved ones who'd died at Carl's hands.

He collapsed onto his cot, resting his back for the first time all day. "Ahh."

"Enjoy while it lasts, butcher."

"Blackjack," Carl corrected. "Butcher was Herbie Sloan. You and your pals got him at Megnus IV. Doubt he would have warranted a festival even if he'd made it back."

"Shut your f-f-f-face!"

They had picked guards who spoke English, but they hadn't been briefed on creative cursing. A couple of the night shift guys were improving. He'd suggested they check the omni and up their game, and to his surprise they seemed to be doing better at wishing pain, suffering, and humiliation on him.

"Yeah, yeah. I know your orders though, Fluffy. I'm supposed to show up at the Six Deaths in pristine condition. Otherwise, you might steal some of the f-f-f-fun." He couldn't help needling the guards' difficulties with that particular English sound.

He was past the point of trying to make nice. Powerless cogs in a military-industrial machine, it would have taken half the prison's staff to enact any kind of escape plan. He was four stories underground. Everything was P-tech, rendering it hack-proof. The guards wore armor including studded gloves, but none carried so much as a knife for a sidearm. Nothing he could steal to enact his own escape. And the staffing was way more than his mere presence warranted, at least from a security standpoint.

Instead, Carl just denied them all the satisfaction of seeing him miserable.

Carl Who Enjoyed Being Notorious was having a field day.

He ate the food they spat in.

He slept on the slab that hurt his back.

He shit in a corner of his cell where a grate too small for any hope of an egress got hosed clean every few days.

He admitted to every crime they attributed to him.

Sure, they'd beaten him pretty good, especially early on. But now that he was a Very Important Prisoner and the highlight of a week-long extravaganza of societal vengeance against Earth Navy, he was a fatted calf being prepped for slaughter, and he planned to go out with a smirk.

"I'm going to enjoy watching your tongue get pulled out in shreds."

Ignoring that vivid image, Carl pressed, "You guys consider a partnership with GNN to simulcast to Earth territory? Especially the Parade of Sorrow. Frankly, you guys give me a lot more credit than I ever got from my own people. I was already the all-time kills leader, but I wouldn't mind padding that record a little. You know, in case some future hotshot comes along with a longer war and fewer politics in his way."

"Don't you *ever* grow weary of-f-f-f your own voice?"

"Nah. I hit the thrust reverse once in a while around the fam, just to give them a rest, but I don't have any reason to take pity on you sorry shits."

A low growl rumbled in the back of his guard's throat.

Knowing he was protected until the time for his public execution arrived, Carl sauntered up to the bars and leaned against them. "C'mon, Fido. I'm twice your age with room to spare, and I was a starfighter pilot, not a marine. Come in here and take your best shot."

"You think I'm stupid..."

"You're a military prison guard. The thought hadn't crossed my mind that you weren't."

"You think you can provoke me into getting myself-f-f-f brought up on insubordination..."

"From what I've seen of your legal system, I think you'd have a case."

"You think you are SO clever..."

"Indisputable fact. Hell, your own media is making me look like Audie Murphy. Yeah. You've never heard of him. Go educate yourself. You'll see what I—Hey. What are you doing?" Carl asked this despite clear evidence that the eyndar guarding him was unbuckling his belt in preparation to remove—or at least lower—his pants. "I don't know what you're planning, but I've got a wife and between four and forty kids, and you're not my—"

"Shut up," the guard ordered.

As Carl backed away from the bars, a golden stream arced through the air. With only about two meters to work with, he was the proverbial barrel-dwelling fish.

After attempting to dodge and failing repeatedly, Carl just relented and stood there. "Ha. Ha. They're going to smell it on me, you know. They'll know it was you."

"It's going to be all of us, once I pass the word around."

Despite his intent to remain upbeat just to piss them all off, he was finding it hard in the face of being the one that they all pissed on.

It was promising to be a long night.

Astral space was still too gray for her liking. Jessie watched the control panel of Grosstet's Shuttle 1, perched on her human ergonomic adapter seat and interpreting standard units that she knew the machinery was converting from haathee equivalents at some unknown level of accuracy.

"Hey, relax, the hard part was getting off the ship," Hadrian told her. "I let Trebla in on the secret of my identity on the off chance it came down to a vote of no confidence in you. No way that walking shower clog was going to stab me in the back knowing the dirt I have on him. But here we are. Eight point whatever-the-hell-you-said astral units deep, and... we've got to be nearly to our destination by now. Don't we?"

Jessie peered at the ever-changing numbers on the readouts. "Yeah," she replied distractedly.

"Well, say the word, and I'll have us—"

"The word is WAIT. You may think your end of this deal is handled, but mine requires some fucking finesse. I've got to match course and speed with a tumbling planet that's outside our direct frame of reference, using maps we stitched together ourselves, then ballpark the rate of our astral re-entry so we don't go off course while we transition."

"But... you'll still have to say the word. I'm fine waiting. I've got the patience of a pyramid."

Jessie didn't take her eyes off the console. "And probably just as many grave robbers in you."

Hadrian laughed. "Probably."

The haathee computers were smart as hell. Jessie didn't even know who'd taught this shuttle astral navigation, but it was providing her course and speed corrections in realtime as she aimed for the wastewater station. She'd baked in a four-second buffer as her best estimate of their transit down to this depth.

She got Shuttle 1 lined up...

Their course was locked in...

She had a countdown to her four-second buffer...

"Get ready... bring us back in three... two... one... NOW!"

Instantly, off-hue astral gave way to an explosion of seawater in the cabin with them.

Unprepared for the deluge, Jessie sucked in a lungful of water before she even realized what was happening.

Efficient haathee life support vents took the excessive humidity in stride, sucking out water by the hundreds of liters a second without needing to be told. Breaking free of the buckles securing her in the pilot's chair, Jessie broke the surface, desperately coughing out brackish water and gasping for air.

As the water receded and Jessie continued to hack up the puddles clinging stubbornly to her insides, a hand patted her on the back.

Panting for breath, Jessie finally glanced up to find Hadrian calm—and perfectly dry—beside her.

"You missed."

"I missed?" Jessie shot back. "What happened to a four-second slide between realspace and astral?"

"You were counting? I was aiming for a rough 8 AU. Takes a little squinting and metaphysical wiggling. Any damned fool can find realspace. You said 'now' and I 'nowed.'"

Climbing back into her chair, soaked to the bones inside and out, Jessie scanned the console. "Let's see where we ended up."

She'd requested Earth-equivalent maps, since too much eyndar was gibberish and she didn't know any local geography before the mission. As it turned out, she didn't know Earth geography a whole lot better.

"We're in something called the Øresund," she stated with some trepidation and an assumption that the first letter sounded like an "O."

"A straight between Sweden and Denmark. I could pilot us there myself from this close... if I knew the first, second, and twentieth things about operating a flying elephant box. And if the eyndar didn't dump so much shit in their oceans that it's thick as three-bean soup."

Now that he mentioned it, the seawater *did* smell a lot different than on most colonies. "Ugh. Lemme get nav onto local realspace and get us moving. I can get a full set of antibiotics when we get back to the *Arete*."

"Good. Wasting enough time as it is."

"Excuse me, but we just threw a dart the equivalent of Luna to Earth, through re-entry, wind, and local disturbances, and still hit the dartboard. Sorry I missed the bullseye."

"Apology accepted, now let's get moving. All those fancy holographic predictions were time-sensitive, as I recall."

Jessie set them on a course and opened the throttle as wide as she dared. The last thing they needed right now was to raise an alarm before they even parked Shuttle 1. "I didn't think you were paying attention in the briefing."

"I have facets of attention you couldn't begin to dream of."

Jessie scoffed. "I think I can at *least* begin."

Every counterintuitive fact about the eyndar homeworld bore out along the undersea voyage. They encountered no commercial fishing—the water was barren of anything big enough to eat. They encountered no recreational divers—the water was too hazardous to play in. The whole ocean seemed to be just a bacteriological cesspit for their entire civilization.

While the planet's own version of Luna provided tides, Jessie piloted against a current that was entirely artificial.

Shuttle 1 jetted upstream against a head current of filth. Proximity sensors alerted them when they'd entered a pipe. The front window now displayed a holographic overlay in place of a pointless transparent look into the zero-visibility water.

A greenscale rendering of a sewage pipe disappeared before them.

Ducts branched. Jessie followed a wider pipe as they backtracked to a manifold that dispersed the waste of the capital city over a wider area of the sea floor.

Eventually, they came to an underground cistern with a giant agitator blade spinning at three or so revolutions per minute. Shuttle 1 was almost certainly able to shrug off a blow from the blade, *probably* tough enough to survive getting wedged between the blade and the edge of the outlet pipe, and one hundred percent maneuverable enough to avoid the clumsy thing if Jessie was paying the slightest bit of attention.

Shuttle 1 broke free of the water, and Jessie set them down away from the gushing pipes that belched fresh toilet leavings and drainage runoff into the cistern.

They landed with a gentle thud.

"Game time."

Hadrian smirked. "Like old times."

———

Jessie exited the shuttle in the lead after Hadrian magically dried both their costumes and Jessie's tactical outfit. Once they stepped onto solid ground, a command from her TeleJack closed up Shuttle 1 and autopiloted it back below the wastewater's surface.

"I indulge this for the sake of your pantomime," Hadrian called out from inside his mask. To all outward appearances, the pair were eyndar visitors to the homeworld with the galaxy's worst parking skills. Hooded cool-suit coats hid their lack of fur. Shoulder pads altered their apparent posture. The design of the masks was meant to hug the stubby eyndar snout and shield sensitive eyes from the pollutants in the homeworld's sky.

None of this junk had been hard to come by. Surplus depots sold it on colonies along both sides of the border.

And the efficacy of their disguises drew a test immediately.

"*You cannot be in here,*" a worker in a full environmental suit shouted as he approached. "*I don't care who told you otherwise.*"

Jessie wasted no time.

She closed the gap in a flash. One blow cracked the worker's neck. A quick twist and a shove, and he toppled over the chain of an inadequate safety barricade and splashed into the sewage.

Hadrian grunted as his long strides caught up easily. "Bet this whole place would go up in flames at the drop of a—"

"Just don't."

"Fine. Fine. Parting gift, maybe. Grosstet's flying lunchpail is fireproof—or as fireproof as one could expect, I imagine."

"Don't imagine anything of the sort. We want to escape without being noticed. Barring that, we want to escape in chaos. What we *don't* need is to drag the chaos along behind us like a trail of exploding breadcrumbs."

"Funny you should mention—"

Jessie whirled and shot the wizard such a glare that it conveyed her ire from behind dark-tinted goggles.

"Another time. Right. Onward. Though I will say, I think the guy who had my mask before me liked fish."

"Blame the seawater," Jessie advised.

"Wasn't exactly the kind of water conducive to fish, if you know what I mean."

Jessie pulled up short. "Hey. Are you in or out? If you're

going to yammer the whole time, you can sit in the shuttle and wait for me to get back with Carl."

Hadrian tucked his gloved hands into the sleeves of his coat, a feat Jessie would have been hard-pressed to believe possible short of magic. "Look here, young lady. I've been at this a long time. A long, LONG time. I've killed more people than you've met. I've rescued your father more times than you've remembered his birthday. There's a better than fifty-fifty chance he doesn't need a rescue. But we rush off because we care and we can't risk the coin falling the wrong way. When we get him out, he'll joke and play it off like he had it under control, even if he was otherwise doomed. That's the trust he puts in the people who love him. We go in there all serious and needy-eyed and desperate, we'll ruin the whole thing."

"You think this is a game?"

"Life is a game. I play to win, dammit, but if you can't enjoy the chance to do right by your friends and punish your enemies, what's the point of it all?"

Jessie didn't have a great answer. How could she argue? Mordecai The Brown. The old-timers on the *Mobius*, who'd flown with Dad since before he got together with Mom, talked about the guy only when drunk. But even now, decades later, there were footprints in the sand that no tide could wash away. Aunt Tiffany was the biggest badass Jessie had ever met. A role model, aside from the magical training. And here was the guy who had not only *given* that training, but who considered the Convocation's top wizard-hunter a nuisance.

"You'd better not fuck this up playing around," was the best she came up with.

"Who are you!?" some poor eyndar fucker demanded as the pair rounded a corner to come face to face with an unmasked sewage worker.

Jessie was about ready to break another neck and look for a

place to stuff a body when the guy just up and disappeared. There was a crackle of flame and a puff of smoke that remained in the air a few seconds afterward, but that was the only hint that there had ever been anyone there in the first place.

"That... that was an illusion, right?" Jessie asked, shaken. "There was... I mean... You're just messing with me to prove a point. He wasn't really...?"

"There one second. Gone the next. And I didn't send him forward in time like I've heard Eric's done. That guy's not coming back. Ever. Don't accuse *me* of fucking this up, pilot. I did more to raise that father of yours than your worthless grandparents ever did."

As they made their way through the sewage facility and up toward the surface, she heard Hadrian warn under his breath, "And if you ever call me 'grandpa,' I swear I'll turn your hair blue."

———

The city streets of This Is Here bustled with Mardi Gras energy, minus the whimsy. Eyndar music reminiscent of yodeling brought back dusty old memories of Carson Colony campfire sing-alongs. Darkness reigned in the sky far overhead, but technological lighting beat it back with iron lamp posts and spiderwebs of colored bistro lights spanning the gaps between concrete buildings.

But the colors were all blues and yellows and browns. The festival was the kind of place that ancient Soviet gulags would have found too depressing.

Mort followed in Jessie's wake as she led them through streets she'd no doubt memorized. Good kid. Did her homework when she cared, and this was a topic she cared about deeply. However, due to the crowds and the celebration, police had cordoned off roads and walkways, funneling foot traffic along prescribed routes.

"Move. Move. Move," a civil defense soldier ordered, sweeping an arm repeatedly to herd the crowd forward. The flow of eyndar revelers carried them off in a direction other than toward the prison.

Jessie turned and tried to make eye contact through the goggles of their masks.

Yeah. No shit this wasn't the plan.

Towering vid boards replayed a loop of Carl center stage at a kangaroo trial, shackled in place as the testimonials of so-called "victims" assailed him. The lad was putting on a brave face, but it was put on. Mort knew him too well not to see it. Some false face. Some discordant belief at the fore. A backstory he forced himself to live as if it had been his life all along.

Notorious?

Cold-blooded?

Oblivious?

Whatever persona the lad had concocted, it looked to be holding up just fine. Captioned commentary on the feed indicated that the presenters were none too impressed with their human captive.

Presently, Mort was none too impressed with the planning abilities of Jessie's crew.

She yanked him aside and out of line. The traffic proceeded without them as the pair entered a chain restaurant just off the main thoroughfare that co-branded itself Slurp'n'Burp in border colonies where the species mixed... at least prior to the last war. Mort couldn't recall the last time he'd seen one with that amusing sign above its door. This one had the standard eyndar branding and a name that translated more literally as Bowl Chow.

"Hungry?" Jessie asked quietly in badly accented eyndar.

Mort was. But he also knew better than to take his mask off to eat straight from a bowl with no silverware. He doubted that the eyndar-exclusive version of the place carried so much as plastic chopsticks to humor human customers.

They got in line, and after advancing two spaces toward the ordering counter, Jessie pointed a gloved fist toward the sign above a side hall. There was an image in icon simplicity of a clearly male eyndar with an arc of urine streaming from a member the size of a stubby limb.

With a nod, Mort followed Jessie out of line and down said hallway. No doors. No separators. Not even its own room. The hall was just wide enough for patrons to walk past a line of festival revelers relieving themselves into an open trough. Jostling and bumping, they made their way through the line of returning, bladder-light eyndar without a hint of a sink or faucet in sight.

Out the far end of the hall, they emerged onto a side street.

Mort followed when Jessie beckoned with a jerk of her head.

Fewer eyndar were on these roads, but their good fortune didn't last. Though they got back on track for the prison, street by street, the crowds grew, and the festive atmosphere turned to fury.

Whether Jessie could make out the words or not, a chant had broken out among a mob surrounding the prison, and Mort understood it just fine. Direct translation could be iffy in eyndar, but the sentiment came across loud and clear.

No justice without blood.

At first, it seemed an odd choice of protest. After all, after another day of public haranguing, they'd get around to the public hanging. Scanning the homemade placards, however, the ludicrous premise crystallized.

These crazy fuckers were upset that day one of the Six

Deaths would just be repeated near-drownings, chained in place in a dunk tank of ever-changing depth, controlled by experienced doctors. Followed, of course, by one actual drowning, whereupon the aforementioned victim would be revived for the next day of torment.

However, the protesters demanded blood. Literal, red, leaking blood. And they were blocking access to the prison in their ire.

Jessie paused at the outskirts of the crowd.

Hadrian placed a hand on her shoulder, and when she turned, he gave a nod and led the way forward.

Magic worked in mysterious ways. As one of the galaxy's foremost experts, even Mort couldn't explain the details half the time. Some of it just... worked.

Concealed in a mask, no one could see his terrible visage.

Bundled in a coat, the eyndar protesters couldn't even identify him as another species.

Cloaked in rage, they somehow sensed that they had no mortal business impeding him.

Mort used an aura of purpose as his bulldozer and plowed forward, cutting through the throng. He didn't look back, trusting that Jessie's sense of purpose rivaled his own and that she wouldn't allow herself to be left behind.

At the steps, armed prison guards kept the protest at bay. A flick of Mort's wrist carried no magic but that of supreme arrogance and entitlement. He dismissed the guards' feeble attempts to ascertain his identity or purpose inside. Clearly offworld dignitaries, someone of higher rank could deal with them inside.

"State your business," a prison bureaucrat instructed brusquely.

Mort's eyndar was impeccable, even if his accent leaned Back Bay Bostonian. "We're here to see the human."

The front door had never been the plan. But the side serviceways had all been sealed by security forces preventing the mob from squeezing into the prison from all sides. Now, Jessie had to trust Mort's improvisational skills.

"There are no visitors allowed. Only guards and medical staff are permitted access. Begone."

Mort loosened his mask. He pulled it down such that his eyes met those of the astonished administrator before she could raise an alarm. "Make an exception."

Canine eyes glazed over. Pupils shrank all the way shut. "Yes. I will. Summon. An escort."

She tapped on a console behind the desk.

Two uniformed guards armored like kids at a martial arts tournament approached the front desk.

"These two. Take them down. They will see the human."

"Reckro, you doing all right?" one asked.

"I. Am fine. Follow my. Orders."

"I hear; I obey," the second guard chimed in. "But you need to request a howling day once the festival is done. The mob outside is getting to you."

"Come on," the first guard cajoled. "You might want to keep the masks on. Lots of people don't handle the smell down below."

Bracketed front and back, Mort and Jessie headed down a squared spiral stairwell of science-stone blocks. Pale, inadequate gizmolight lent an air of despair befitting a dungeon.

Down, down they went.

Hand signals. Key rings. Clunky mechanical locks. The eyndar employed an admirable lack of modern pretension to their prison facility.

Halfway down, a commotion rose.

Panicked eyndar shouts of confusion revealed nothing but a security breach in progress.

"Shall we?" Mort asked in plain English.

"Huh?" a guard inquired as the pair herded Mort and Jessie out of the way as booted feet raced up from below.

Jessie gave a nod.

The jig was up.

Mort waved a hand. Harsh, demonic runes flashed inside his skull. The two guards were gone.

Pulling off the mask and tucking it under one arm, he led the way onward.

"Do you know where you're going?" Jessie demanded, now lugging her mask as spare baggage as well.

Rather than answer in words, Mort stepped aside and allowed her to take point.

"Intruder!"

"Sound the alarm!"

"Lock down the building!"

"So much for getting to him first," Jessie griped, breaking into a run that slowed only to punch and kick steel-barred doors that blocked their path.

Mort, despite lungs and legs belonging to a much younger man, jogged and lagged, vaporizing dead bodies out of pique and spite and the off chance that any of Jessie's victims along the path to Carl's cell still clung to life.

"No... NO!!!" Jessie wailed.

Mort soon saw the reason for her distress.

The bodies of guards meant nothing to either of them.

Jessie knelt over the still, lifeless form of Carl Ramsey on the floor of his cell.

This wasn't happening.

"Wake up. WAKE UP!" Jessie shook her father, but the burnt hole in his chest rendered any hope of him faking remote. She turned, eyes pleading, as Hadrian entered the cell behind her. "Figure out the trick. A clone? A dummy? Is this some dead eyndar they made to look like him?"

Hadrian shook his head solemnly. "I'm sorry, old friend. I never expected it to... Well, that's not true. I suppose you avoided this fate so many times, I took for granted you were out of the woods."

"He's still warm. Maybe we can... can you do anything?"

Hadrian sighed. "Maybe Harmony."

Jessie's mind raced. Right. Harmony. Magic could perform miracles, but this wasn't the time for wishful thinking. They had access to science with proven history of reaching past the veil and fishing out souls from the well of infinity. "We'll have to be quick. I don't know how long someone can be... can be..." She couldn't get the word past her lips.

"Can you carry him?"

It was a long way back to the shuttle. She gathered Dad up in her arms. He was skinnier than he used to be, back in his harder-drinking days, but he was still a grown-ass man and around ninety kilos. Hoisting him over a shoulder, Jessie turned her thoughts inward, reminding herself of Master Bentho's teachings.

Pain is in the mind.

Muscles are tools of the mind.

Clear all nonessential thoughts, and the mind can achieve what it cannot believe.

"I think so. I don't know how we're getting past that mob outside though."

"I do."

Despite grief and despair that no amount of meditative

clarity could stamp out, Jessie found the wizard's manner chilling.

"Stay behind me. Well behind if you're not worried about getting lost. And if you can whistle and call that flying beer can to meet us, do it."

"How much magic are you planning to use?" Jessie asked, suddenly concerned that their quick getaway might be delayed indefinitely by technological failure.

"All. Of. It."

There was no arguing. Jessie gulped, nodded, and followed.

Despite the commotion, the lockdown, the guards racing in panic at the loss of a highly valued prisoner, no one got past Hadrian.

Steel doors cooled in molten puddles as she hopped past.

Screams of terror kept her from losing track of the wizard, though they were both backtracking their route in.

The front doors to the prison were gone. Fleeing eyndar protesters wailed their own dirges as flames clung to them stubbornly, slowly and horrifically counting down the ends of their lives.

Shifting Dad's weight, Jessie managed to access her TeleJack and contact Shuttle 1. She tapped in a course back out through the Øresund and skyward to meet them.

"Shuttle's en route. Could use a distraction so no one shoots it down." Jessie knew Grosstet's shuttle was a tough little nut, but she couldn't bank solely on that. Plus, they'd be vulnerable boarding.

"One distraction... coming up."

Jessie felt the heat rise and turned, wide-eyed, to find the prison engulfed in flames.

Not "someone threw an improvised combustible grenade" in flames, but "holy hell, the entire structure made of permacrete blocks is on fire." And not just on fire, but melting in the heat. A building that probably would have taken a marine platoon hours to level with disintegrator rifles and microatomic rockets was dripping like a birthday candle.

And Mort wasn't done.

Civil defense patrol ships caught fire on flybys.

A vortex over the plaza with all the vid boards gathered portable chairs and tables, trash bins, chunks of permacrete from the road, window glass, and bricks as the nearby buildings crumbled, and hundreds of screaming, terrified eyndar revelers.

Into the air they fell as if a new star was born, and fusion turned the whole mass into a nuclear bowling ball that Hadrian launched into the imperial palace at the plaza's far end.

Jessie found herself agape.

Amid this headlong collision of grief and madness, the streetlamps across from the prison hadn't so much as blinked.

Jessie coughed, remembering that this was no place to be breathing the local air, but discovered that she'd left her mask down inside the now-molten prison.

When Shuttle 1 swooped in and opened a ramp for them, oblivious to the chaos into which it had flown, Hadrian had to help her load Dad aboard.

Hacking and gasping, she managed to raise the ramp behind them.

"Deep breath," Hadrian told her, demonstrating.

Jessie fought the urge to take quick, panicked gasps between coughs.

"Aaaaaand... exhale."

One huge cough expelled a cloud of smoke that felt like it inverted her lungs on the way out.

Other than raw and burning, her lungs felt otherwise fine.

"Warned you not to breathe that shit. Talk to Master Bentho next time you see him; he'll teach you the trick. For now, buckle up. We're taking the short way back to the *Arete*."

Before Jessie made it halfway to the cockpit, the universe disappeared under her feet.

━━━

The *Arete's* holotheater had subdivided the giant 3D field into four different newsfeeds from eyndar territory. Each was covering current developments on a story that seemed impossible to believe.

On Dread Moon Network, they had orbital coverage of a fire raging in the imperial capital. Victorious Armada Square was an open-air charnel house. The imperial palace had been leveled by some kind of experimental weapon, and a hot-ion bomb had melted the very walls of the prison where Blackjack Ramsey was being held.

Right beside that coverage, on the Bloodfang Clan Official Newsfeed, a pair of eyndar women chatted amiably about the extended pageantry of the Six Deaths Festival and the elaborate military simulation running during the celebration, proving the might of the Eyndar Empire and the fear they brought to all who opposed them.

An anonymized feed from a local subversive journalist on the ground scraped bits and pieces of footage together from primary sources. Through a scrambler, he narrated the devastation taking place in the capital city. In one of the clips, a blurry purple-silver brick swooped in, collected a blurry payload, and raised an indistinct ramp before zooming off. The lack of focus was all the more glaring when every other bit of the holo was crisp and clear.

And, lastly, mostly for lack of a fourth informative option, the holo-projector carried the Eyndar Imperial Word, the state-sanctioned official truth. Their narrative was reliant entirely on clips from the victims' shaming of Carl earlier that day.

According to the "true" version of events, technical difficulties with the apparatus for the First Death were causing a pause in the proceedings.

All of this, of course, relied on realtime text and voice translation, which made a lot of the Eyndar Empire's shit sound kind of pompous and stupid. But since most of the crew spoke a smattering of the language at best, and fewer could read it, the translations seemed best for everyone.

"You think that blur was them?" Jasmine asked, pointing with a handful of popcorn in her fist toward the subversive feed.

Trebla huffed a sigh and shrugged. "Wizards are usually invisible to cameras. So, that tracks. But you know what else doesn't show up on holocam? Actual nothingness."

Mindy and Daphne arrived together bearing a basket of barbecue ribs from the saloon and took seats just in front of the pair. "Latest and greatest, luvs? Catch us up?"

"Lies, confusion, fire..." Jasmine replied.

"Plus a lot of blurry footage," Trebla added.

Daphne couldn't tear her eyes from the subversive newsfeed. "I'm not used to watching for history to happen because I helped plan it."

Trebla munched his popcorn, trying his best not to develop a serious case of meat envy. "On the off chance that Hadrian did half that shit we're seeing, I'm being a lot nicer to that guy when he gets back."

"Is it weird that seeing that carnage is almost enough to make me consider a human?" Jasmine asked no one in particular.

"No," Daphne answered.

Mindy grunted. "Or a fella."

"I'm OK just thinking of him as a friend," Trebla stated for the record.

"Good," Sparta called out as she made her way down the rows toward them. She wore leggings and a baggy, cable-knit white turtleneck sweater that screamed "I came from the auto-loom this morning," though she matched her comfy attire with every bit of jewelry she apparently owned. "He's still mine and I can still twist you lot into pretzels to keep him. Not that I expect I'd have to." She glanced around. "Really? Refreshments? At a time like this?"

Mindy replied with her mouth full. "Gal's gotta eat, don't she?"

Sparta studied the feeds a moment. "Not a bit of that looks according to plan."

"Says the oracle," Trebla teased. "Nice work. Care to pitch us an ending? Charlotte nixed the betting pools, so Logistics isn't making predictions."

Jasmine elbowed him. "I'm sure they're going to be fine."

Sparta watched as the Dread Moon Network interrupted with breaking news: Emperor Grudrak was confirmed dead in the palace attack. Emperor Kelgruuk was expected to address the Eyndar Empire shortly.

"Of course, they're going to be fine," Sparta stated emphatically. "Hadrian controls his fate." She glanced down at the bucket of ribs. "Real or saloon?"

"Saloon," Daphne answered.

Sparta pointed silently to Jasmine and Trebla's popcorn.

"Real. There's a machine up back that makes it," Jasmine replied. Sparta made no move, waiting expectantly, presumably for an offer to share. Jasmine handed the paper carton to Trebla. "How about I come help make us *both* a fresh batch?"

"Never expected I'd see that one all knotted up," Mindy remarked softly once the popcorn-seeking pair was out of earshot. "Can only imagine how the other one's managing."

Trebla scrunched his brow as he paused in searching for

fully popped kernels at the bottom of the carton. "Huh? Other one what? OHHHH! You mean Eric. Nah, Charlotte's probably holding his hand in the arboretum or some shit."

"Hardly," Mindy scoffed. "Just off bridge duty, and she was up there the whole of it. Still on for a double, on account of ain't nobody cuttin' the queue for therapy on a day like this. No point prunin' the old trauma tree until you know what branches we all got growin'."

"I wonder if we started a war," Daphne murmured as coverage on the Eyndar Imperial Word shifted from stonewall denials to lavish praise for the new emperor and speculation on how he might handle reprisals for this attack.

Mindy glanced over to where Jasmine was giving a longwinded and pointless lesson in corn popping to a wizard who was leaking P-tech out both ears faster than she listened. "Mark my words. Ain't enough popcorn in the galaxy for what's coming next."

⸻

Eric fidgeted, barely able to concentrate on the game.

"I-still-do-not-have-any-sevens-Go-fish."

Go Fish was his selection each time the "dealer's choice" came around to him. The others all chose various forms of draw and stud poker, but Eric earned a little leeway for being willing to play with ratatoret-sized cards. He used a fingertip to spread the common ones before selecting his pick from the middle and enlisting help from someone with tiny claws to get under it and lift it from the hangar floor.

Tiny datapad alerts blared from all around the circle. The ratatoret players—all members of the Logistics Division— scrambled to their feet and scattered. Only Chinochin lingered long enough to offer an explanation.

"Shuttle-1-is-inbound-They-have-retrieved-your-father-but-are-looking-for-prompt-transport-to-Med-Bay-I-don't-have-any-further-information-for-you-and-must-attend-to—"

"Yeah, yeah," Eric cut in, waving him off. "Go ahead. I'll just clean up here."

Heart pounding, Eric swept up the tiny cards using magic that would have been rude *during* the game. He guided the stacks of chips used during the more gambling-friendly rounds at one side of the aisle of the warehouse that their game had been blocking.

As he stared, the floor aperture irised open. Through the blue haze of the force field, Grosstet's shuttle rose, caked in gunk, and zipped over the heads of the team preparing to receive them near Shuttle 1's usual parking spot.

Lift doors opened around the time the shuttle got its ramp open.

Eric was already running.

Arms flailing.

Feet flapping.

Tears streaming.

This was some kind of emergency, and his only blood relatives around here were aboard that shuttle.

Something must have gone wrong.

Hadrian couldn't fly. That meant either Dad or Jessie was worried about the other, and Eric's heart couldn't take it either way.

Britney and Harmony had a hover stretcher. Jessie flopped Dad onto it and followed the pair back into the lift.

Eric just managed to jump through the doors before they shut.

"What happened Is he OK He doesn't look OK But you've fixed worse than that right Harmony Of course you have everything is going to be fine I just know it But if you need anything blood hair liver samples I'm your guy Since we're related he's probably my liver type That's where that hole is right Somewhere around the liver Is he breathing He doesn't look like he's breathing I—"

"Eric," Jessie stated firmly. "Shut up. Let Harmony work."

Harmony was a flurry of handheld doodads. "No vitals. No heart rate. No brain activity. How long has he been like this? Based on body temperature, no more than an hour or two."

"We made it back in fifteen minutes," Jessie replied. "Most of it was just the nav computer having an existential crisis."

The lift ride ended so suddenly that Eric almost missed exiting as the others rushed off with Dad on the stretcher, Britney pushing.

"You can do this," Jessie told their doctor friend. "You've brought back so many people since we—"

"This is different," Harmony snapped as they got into Med Bay. "Minutes, not hours." She hooked up scanners from an examination bed once they transferred Dad onto it. He looked like hell; there was no getting around it.

"I trust you," Jessie reassured Harmony from a respectful pace away, allowing room for the medical team to work.

"Zero deep brain function. Microcellular decay has set in. Prep a restart sequence. We'll deal with the damage once we revive him."

Thingies stuck all over Dad's body. They pushed buttons, and he convulsed. But it wasn't him doing the convulsions; the science was doing it to him.

Eric stood outside himself, behind his own eyes, watching through foggy windows as a scene less real than anything in the Village of Eternity unfolded. A ritual so bizarrely modern. A patient so out of his usual character.

A doctor so frustrated and hopeless.

"Jessica... I'm sorry."

Tears streamed down his sister's face. "Hadrian only started avenging you. I'll finish the job. I swear. I SWEAR! The Eyndar Empire is OVER! We're setting a course. Planet by planet. Hit and run. Every space station. Every dung-farming colony. Every—"

"Jess..."

The two women looked over. Eric saw them staring before he realized they were staring AT him.

Still struggling to hold back full-on sobs, Jessie opened her arms and came toward him.

She was a zombie of grief, and if she reached him, he'd catch it too.

Curling into a ball, Eric shouted his denial. "No! NO! NOOOOO!"

A fork fell with a clatter that rang through the dining lounge.

⸻

IT ALL STARTS HERE

Eric held perfectly still.

He was seated.

This was the dining lounge.

These were his strawberry pancakes with butter and syrup.

Dad didn't die in the Eyndar Empire. He couldn't. Any timeline where that might happen simply wasn't real.

But Eric remembered.

On the off chance that he'd passed out and simply woken up in the same place, Eric abandoned both the fork and his meal. Racing through the ship, he found Jessie in her quarters.

"What?" she demanded when the door opened. "You know I'm busy." She wagged a datapad in case he didn't know what busy was supposed to look like.

Rather than accept its presence as a simple prop, Eric snatched away the datapad and checked the date. He was no expert on datapads, but they usually had the date and time up top if they didn't have pressing business using the whole screen.

19 JULY 2592

"Hey!" Jessie grabbed her device back. But her ire was cut short when Eric threw his arms around her.

"I didn't mess up! I did it! We're going to save him!"

Arms far stronger than his own gave a quick, affectionate pat before prying him loose. "Great to hear. Now get lost. I've got intel to scrape together and every second could count."

"Oh! Right. No. You don't know how right you are. Carry on, Jess. Carry on."

She shook her head. "You are *so* strange."

The door slid shut between them.

Eric bounded away with a grin on his face. He had two days to change Jessie and Hadrian's mission from a failure to a Dad-saving success!

Black Ocean

Black Ocean is a vivid 26th century story universe where science and magic coexist—sort of.

Black Ocean: Galaxy Outlaws (16 missions)

Black Ocean: Galaxy Outlaws is a fast-paced fantasy space opera series about the small crew of the *Mobius* trying to squeeze out a living. If you love fantasy and sci-fi, and still lament over the cancellation of *Firefly*, *Black Ocean: Galaxy Outlaws* is the series for you.

Read about the *Black Ocean: Galaxy Outlaws* series and discover where to buy at: galaxyoutlawsmissions.com

Black Ocean: Astral Prime (12 missions)

Co-written with author M.A. Larkin, *Black Ocean: Astral Prime* hearkens back to location-based space sci-fi classics like *Babylon 5* and *Star Trek: Deep Space Nine*. *Astral Prime* builds on the rich *Black Ocean* universe, introducing a colorful cast of characters for new and returning readers alike. Come along for the ride as a minor outpost in the middle of nowhere becomes a key point of interstellar conflict.

Read about the *Black Ocean: Astral Prime* series and discover where to buy at: astralprimemissions.com

Black Ocean: Mercy for Hire (16 missions)

Black Ocean: Mercy for Hire follows the exploits of a pair of do-gooder bounty hunters who care more about saving the day than securing a payday. The series builds on the rich *Black Ocean* universe, centering on a couple of fan-favorites and introducing a colorful cast for new and returning readers alike. Fans of vigilante justice and heroes who exemplify the word will love this series.

Read about *Black Ocean: Mercy for Hire* and discover where to buy at: mercyforhiremissions.com

Black Ocean: Mirth & Mayhem (16 missions)

Black Ocean: Mirth & Mayhem delves into the origins of two vagabonds making their living among the stars. Mort is a wizard coming to grips with a life on the run and estrangement from the comforts and respect he had on Earth. Brad is an impressionable youth, too clever for his—or anyone's—good. And Chuck Ramsey is the mold that Brad's trying to break out of, which is harder than he could ever have dreamed.

Read about *Black Ocean: Mirth & Mayhem* and discover where to buy at: mirthandmayhemmissions.com

Black Ocean: Passage of Time (in-progress)

The year was 2586. A few minutes later, it was 2591. Caught up in a time travel snafu, Eric and Jessie Ramsey become fugitives from the people who want answers as to how they did it—and where their loyalties lie in the galactic war that broke out in their absence.

Read about *Black Ocean: Passage of Time* and discover where to buy at: passageoftimemissions.com

Black Ocean Fan Group

Join the *Black Ocean* Facebook fan group to discuss *Black Ocean* with other outlaws. Chat about ebooks, audio, or paper versions; main series or spin-offs; or share photos of the pet you named after Kubu.

Request to join at: blackoceanfans.com

Black Ocean Merch

Wish you could live in the Black Ocean world?

I can't promise you'll win an argument with the universe, but you CAN wear your own wizard hoodie (adorned with Convocation medallion), disguise your boring 21st-century soda or beer with the Earth's Preferred can cooler, or fly the Poet Fleet Jolly Roger.

Browse merch at: blackoceangear.com

Twinborn Chronicles

The *Twinborn Chronicles* is an epic fantasy saga based on the possibility that our dreams offer us a glimpse into the life of another – another who can get the same glimpse into our world.

Read about the *Twinborn Chronicles* and discover where to buy at: twinbornchronicles.com

Twinborn Chronicles: Awakening

Experience the journey of mundane scribe Kyrus Hinterdale who discovers what it means to be Twinborn—and the dangers of getting caught using magic in a world that thinks it exists only in children's stories.

Twinborn Chronicles: War of 3 Worlds

Then continue on into the world of Korr, where the Mad Tinker and his daughter try to save the humans from the oppressive race of Kuduks. When their war spills over into both Tellurak and Veydrus, what alliances will they need to forge to make sure the right side wins?

Project Transhuman: Eve14

Project Transhuman brings genetic engineering into a post-apocalyptic Earth, 1000 years aliens obliterated all life.

These days, even the humans are built by robots.

Charlie7 is the oldest robot alive. He's seen everything from the fall of mankind at the hands of alien invaders to the rebuilding of a living world from the algae up. But what he hasn't seen in over a thousand years is a healthy, intelligent human. When Eve stumbles into his life, the old robot finally has something worth coming out of retirement for: someone to protect.

Read about all of the *Project Transhuman* books and discover where to buy at: projecttranshuman.com

Sins of Angels

Co-written with author M.A. Larkin, *Sins of Angels* is an epic space opera series set 3000 years after the fall of Earth. With the scope of *Dune* and the adventurous spirit of *Indiana Jones*, it delivers a conflict that spans galaxies and rests on the spirit of brave researcher Professor Rachel Jordan. Follow the complete saga, and watch as the fate of our species hangs in the balance.

Read about *Sins of Angels* and discover where to buy at:
sinsofangelsbooks.com

Shadowblood Heir

Shadowblood Heir explores what would happen if the writer of your favorite epic fantasy TV show died before the show ended—and the show was responsible. If you wonder what it would be like if an epic fantasy world invaded our world, this urban fantasy story might give you that glimpse.

Read about *Shadowblood Heir* and discover where to buy at:
shadowbloodheir.com

EMAIL INSIDERS

You made it to the end! Maybe you're just persistent, but hopefully that means you enjoyed the book. But this is just the end of one story. If you'd like reading my books, there are always more on the way!

Perks of being an Email Insider include:

- Inside track on beta reading and advance review copies (ARCs)
- Access to Inside Exclusive bonus extras and giveaways
- Best of my blog about fantasy and science fiction topics

Sign up for the my Email Insiders list at: jsmorin.com/updates

ABOUT THE AUTHOR

I am a creator of worlds and a destroyer of words. As a fantasy writer, my works range from traditional epics to futuristic fantasy with starships. I have worked as an unpaid Little League pitcher, a cashier, a student library aide, a factory grunt, a cubicle drone, and an engineer—there is some overlap in the last two.

Through it all, though, I was always a storyteller. Eventually I started writing books based on the stray stories in my head, and people kept telling me to write more of them. Now, that's all I do for a living.

I enjoy strategy, worldbuilding, and the fantasy author's privilege to make up words. I am a gamer, a joker, and a thinker of sideways thoughts. But I don't dance, can't sing, and my best artistic efforts fall short of your average notebook doodle. When you read my books, you are seeing me at my best.

Connect with me online
jsmorin.com

facebook.com/authorjsmorin
bookbub.com/authors/j-s-morin
youtube.com/@authorjsmorin

www.ingramcontent.com/pod-product-compliance
Lightning Source LLC
Chambersburg PA
CBHW032007240626
47153CB00003B/1164